W9-CAY-215

STAR WARS

QUEEN'S PERIL

STAR WARS

QUEEN'S PERIL

Written by

E. K. JOHNSTON

DISNEY • LUCASFILM PRESS

LOS ANGELES • NEW YORK

© & TM 2020 Lucasfilm Ltd.

All rights reserved. Published by Disney • Lucasfilm Press,

an imprint of Disney Book Group. No part of this book may be reproduced

or transmitted in any form or by any means, electronic or mechanical,

including photocopying, recording, or by any information storage and

retrieval system, without written permission from the publisher.

For information address Disney • Lucasfilm Press,

1200 Grand Central Avenue, Glendale, California 91201.

Printed in the United States of America

First Edition, June 2020

1 3 5 7 9 10 8 6 4 2

FAC-021131-20115

ISBN 978-1-368-05714-1

Library of Congress Control Number on file

Reinforced binding

Design by Leigh Zieske

Visit the official *Star Wars* website at: www.starwars.com.

SUSTAINABLE FORESTRY INITIATIVE   Certified Sourcing

www.sfiprogram.org
SFI-00993

Logo Applies to Text Stock Only

To Bria and Rachel and Katherine, who, mercifully,

did not ask questions I couldn't answer

The girl in the white dress had her mother's brain and her father's heart, and a spark that was entirely her own. Brilliance and direction and compassion as bright as the stars. But now she was alone, and no one could help her. Whatever happened next, however it was recorded and remembered, she was entirely on her own.

From the time she was small, she had wanted to help. Her father had taken her offworld. She stepped foot on dying planets and tried to hold back the inevitable. Sometimes, it hadn't been enough, but she had always volunteered to try again.

Eventually, she had turned her attention to her own planet. There were no great trials to be faced on Naboo. The sector was at peace, the planet prospering. Yet there was work to be done, work she felt that she could do. And she wanted to do it.

It wasn't enough to settle for her parents' dreams. She wanted to know that she had gone as high as she could, done as much as she was able. And for a girl on Naboo, that meant being elected queen. She was younger than most, but she wasn't about to let that stop her.

The more she looked into it, the more she realized that ruling the planet would be more of a challenge than she thought. The galaxy was a big place, and Naboo was a pretty world without much in the way of defense. The current queen had ignored their neighbors. Their senator was strong, but their list of allies was thin. She knew she was up to the challenge.

And now she waited alone, in a small room in the lower levels of the palace. The campaign was done, the votes were cast. Soon the results would be publicized, and then she would know. But in her heart, she knew already. She always had. She had made herself to serve, and she would do so from the highest possible position.

The door hissed open, and a familiar outline blocked the light. The buzz of a hovering droid filled her ears. The girl straightened. She always acted as though she was being watched. Her appearance was her first line of defense, and she planned to muster it as deliberately as possible.

"Your Highness," Quarsh Panaka said, the faintest ghost of a smile upon his lips. Her captain was still getting to know her, but she trusted his intentions. "The election is over. Your work has begun."

The girl in the white dress was going to be Queen, and she was ready.

STRENGTH

⅃↓⅂⋁⅂⊓⊟

This was not the customary way to receive exam results. The Theed Conservatory attracted students from all over the planet, even though it was hardly the only music school on Naboo. It wasn't even, in public opinion, the best one. Set in an old building, far from any of the main hubs of the city's entertainment, the conservatory was known for its traditions. That was why families sent their children there. A musician trained there was consistent. Steady. Reliable. Ready to pass traditions on to a new generation of listeners and students alike, whether anyone wanted it or not.

Tsabin had hated almost every moment of it.

There had never been any question about where she would be sent. There hadn't even been any question about what instrument she'd play. Her brothers had forged the path ahead of her, and all she had to do was follow along. There was never any question of her doing something so bold as **leading***. She simply didn't have the talent for it. She was good enough, and offworld she might even make a living as a soloist somewhere that didn't know any better, but Tsabin had known for her entire life that she was never going to be in the front row of any orchestra.*

And now she waited in a small room, staring down an empty chair across an unremarkable table. She had been sent there by the proctor droid, barely

*thinking about the unfamiliar room number, expecting to find out how she'd
done on her finals. Instead: a dark room and an endless-seeming wait.*

*Tsabin had made it as far as she had by hiding her true feelings from every-
one, and she wasn't about to crack now, not even for outdated bureaucracy.*

*The door finally opened—really swinging on real hinges, because that was
the sort of place the Theed Conservatory was—and Tsabin straightened in the
chair. Even if it was only the droid, it was important to be ready. Conservatory
droids were known to monitor students' posture and bearing, keeping track of
who was the best at* looking *like a musician, as well as performing mundane
tasks. But the person in the doorway was not a droid. Tsabin took a deep breath
without giving any appearance of doing so, another benefit of a conservatory
education.*

*He was taller than she was, which wasn't saying a lot. It was a place to start,
though. He wore the blue and maroon of the Naboo Royal Security Forces, his
hat tucked under his arm since he was inside. He had short-cropped hair and
dark brown skin, and his eyes were almost warm, except that something around
the edge of him prevented that measure of relaxation. He took the other seat
without introducing himself, and placed the hat on the table between them.*

*If the security officer were hoping to rattle her, he'd picked the wrong day for
it. Exams were over, and Tsabin had gotten a full night's sleep for the first time
in weeks. Her family had all been in touch with her that morning. Her brothers
had reassured her that everything would be fine, and her parents had let her
know where they could be reached when her results were in. She knew she hadn't
done anything to merit this visit, so it must be a curiosity. It must be something
he wanted from her. So Tsabin looked at him calmly, every wall she'd ever built
shielding her from him.*

After several long minutes, the ghost of a smile appeared on his lips, and he stretched a hand across the table toward her, palm up.

"Quarsh Panaka," he said. "Royal Security Forces. But I assume you could tell that for yourself."

"Tsabin," she replied, politely shaking his hand. "Yes."

He let her go, and she returned her hands to her lap. He folded his on the table and looked at her.

"How do you feel about the election?" he asked.

Tsabin raised an eyebrow in spite of herself. She had not expected that question.

"I am not required to tell you," she replied.

"That's true," he said, and almost laughed. "You will at least confirm that you are aware of the candidates?"

"Of course," she said. "This is the first year I get to vote."

"You're thirteen," he said. He leaned back in his chair without losing any sense of being on guard.

"I'll be fourteen by then," she told him. "You must have at least discovered my birthday before you came in here."

"I did," he said. He tapped his fingers on the tabletop.

Tsabin was starting to get annoyed. Yes, it was the first day of the rest of her life—at least in theory, given that her formal education was all but finished—and she didn't exactly have plans, but she also didn't want to waste the day in this room with this man.

"Your teachers say you are diligent," Panaka said. "You are never late. You are scrupulous when it comes to performing your part, and your conduct is near perfect at all times."

Tsabin waited for the other shoe to drop, as it always did.

"And yet you are always second best," Panaka continued. "At everything you have ever tried."

Almost fourteen years of hard-fought control snapped through Tsabin's entire body. She would not give him the satisfaction of seeing how much it hurt. She would never, ever give that to anyone. Her stomach clenched, but she didn't blink or even tighten her jaw at his words. They were, after all, only the truth: her brothers were better musicians than she was, and no matter what she did at the conservatory, there was always someone else who did it better than she.

Panaka stood and picked his hat up off the table.

"I can't say anything officially, of course," he said. "But I would request that you not accept any apprenticeship offers until after the election. I will be in touch."

With those words, he left. Tsabin was free to go. But she reached into her pocket for her screen and pulled up the list of candidates running for Queen of Naboo. She had read their names and their platforms before, but this time, she made herself really look at them. At her.

Amidala, she called herself. *They could be twins, almost. Two girls with the same face. And a security officer had come all the way here to talk to a girl who was always second.*

Tsabin stayed in the room until the droid came looking for her, her mind awake to the possibilities.

CHAPTER 1

The morning of the election, Quarsh Panaka let his tea get cold. His wife, Mariek, fresh off her shift in the palace, suffered no such hesitation, and drank it for him when it became apparent he wasn't going to tear himself away from the screen for anything so mundane as breakfast. She sniped the fresh fruit off his plate as well.

"It's too early to be checking," she pointed out, her mouth full.

"I'm not checking for results," he said.

There hadn't been a true scandal during a Naboo election in decades, but Panaka was not about to let that record be broken on his watch. As a captain in the Royal Security Forces, it was his privilege to ensure that everything went without a hitch. This time it was even more important: the candidate whose protection had been assigned to him was favored to win. Panaka was going to be ready for anything. There were crowds to monitor, and while the Security Forces were more than capable of that, he was curious about what the holonews might catch. It was always best to have as many eyes as possible.

"I'm going to bed," Mariek said.

Panaka did look up at that. She stood, and he took her hand in his. They'd been on opposite shifts ever since he was reassigned to electoral detail in anticipation of what a new monarch might require, and he missed her.

"Sleep well, love," he said.

"Please eat something," she replied, and left him to it.

Panaka dutifully ate three bites off his plate, and he had just decided that maybe he was hungry after all when his private comm sounded.

"Panaka," he said, holding the device in the flat of his palm. The image wavered, and a familiar form appeared in his hand. He straightened. "Senator Palpatine?"

"Good morning, Captain," the senator said.

Usually the Naboo senator returned home to vote, a demonstration to his people and to the Republic that he took all of his roles within the democratic system seriously, but this time he had been kept away by serious business. To be honest, Panaka had missed him. Everything seemed to go more smoothly when the senator was around and always had, even when Panaka was still a clerk in the legislative office and Palpatine's star was on the rise. It was handy to have reliable colleagues.

"I'm sorry to make contact so early," Palpatine continued. "There's a vote later that I can't afford to miss, but I wanted to check in with you today, and I'm afraid that with the time differences, by the time my Senate business dies down, it will be too late."

"It's not a problem, Senator," Panaka replied. "Everything here is going well. The lines are orderly, and the polls open in less than half an hour. All signs point to a smooth election."

"Do they point to a result yet?" Palpatine asked.

Panaka hesitated. Technically, as government officials, they were supposed to discourage speculation. As concerned citizens, however, they were free to discuss their thoughts. Panaka was always careful to keep his work and his private life separate. It was one of the reasons his marriage was so successful.

"Not officially, of course," he said. He picked up his teacup, forgetting Mariek had drained it earlier. "But it appears your hunch was correct. It won't be a scandal if she doesn't win, but it will be a surprise."

As a rule, Naboo queens kept their office for two full terms. However, when Queen Réillata had retired after only one, the planet had to elect a replacement for her before they expected to. There were wonderful candidates, of course—Naboo tradition allowed for nothing else—but the populace had been more fractured in voting than they usually were. Sanandrassa wasn't a bad queen, but she didn't have the support a ruling monarch should expect. Her reelection was, at best, a long shot.

"Good, good," Palpatine said. His gaze flickered away

from Panaka's. Something on Coruscant must have drawn his attention. "I look forward to seeing this through, Captain. In the meantime, I do apologize, but the new taxation bills have finally been transmitted and they require my attention."

"Of course, Senator," Panaka replied. "Thank you for calling."

Palpatine disconnected without any further comment, and Panaka flipped his holo back to the news screens. It was always like that with them: work first. Panaka found it comforting. There was never any doubt about where he stood.

His chronometer chimed, indicating that it was later than he'd thought. Mariek had voted early, and Panaka had gone with her but hadn't cast his own ballot yet. He loved Election Day, and his duties didn't start until midafternoon, so he was free to vote at a regular poll. Whistling happily—a song that had been stuck in his head since he left the conservatory—he put his dishes in the cleaner, made sure he had the proper identification in his pocket, found his boots, and headed out to make a difference.

𝟕𝗩𝗩𝟕

Ruwee Naberrie brushed the sawdust off his vest and wondered where in his life he had gone wrong. Usually he would take a moment to watch the falling wood shavings, evidence of a job done in perfect detail, but today there was no time for that. Today, despite his best efforts, his daughter didn't need him.

She was gone. He hadn't seen her in a few days, except on the holos as she gave last-minute campaign speeches, and then again this morning when she and the other candidates had cast their ballots live for the whole planet to see. It was strange to think about, his youngest trying to be queen of the planet, and he couldn't acknowledge her as such.

People knew, of course. It was impossible to achieve complete anonymity, even with the practiced wheels of Naboo's democratic machine. But no one was going to blow Amidala's cover. Later, if she was successful and if her reign was favorable, her family and friends would explode with pride, but that was for when her term was done. Now Naboo needed a queen.

Ruwee pulled his thoughts back before they could run too far ahead into the future. She might not win the election. She had done very well during the campaign, but that wasn't always an indication of success. Ruwee had left politics behind a long time ago, save when some cause pulled him back in and he made use of his extensive contacts offworld, and he was no stranger to its workings. Things could always turn out unexpectedly.

And, if he was forced to be honest with himself, he almost hoped they would. If she lost, then she could still be herself, without the eyes of hundreds on her every move. Ruwee didn't doubt for a moment that his daughter genuinely wanted to be queen, but it wasn't the hope he'd had for her. He wanted his daughters to be happy, first, and to provide their service to the planet outside of that happiness. Being elected might make her happy, but it would always be tied to something else.

He was still going to vote for her, obviously.

$$\textrm{꓄ ꙮ ꙮ ꛡ}$$

"Ruwee, it's time to go!" Jobal called from inside their well-appointed house.

Unlike her husband, Jobal Naberrie had very few doubts about how this day was going to go, nor did she feel his reluctance at the probable outcome. Their daughter was young, and with the screen around her public life that Naboo tradition would maintain for her, there was no reason at all why she couldn't move on when her time was up. Jobal was deeply proud, of course, and also wildly curious about what her daughter would do. It was a strange feeling, one Ruwee didn't understand at *all*, but Jobal couldn't seem to shake it entirely. It was, she thought, at the very least a good balance for his reservations.

A family holo caught her eye, and Jobal stared at it for a long moment. The image captured Padmé and her sister in the garden as toddlers, carefully weeding ordered rows of vegetables. Padmé had insisted on a kitchen garden and done most of the work herself, sure that the food she produced could be given to people who needed it. Even in a semi-frozen moment in the past, Padmé was a force to be reckoned with. Jobal had known that. She'd seen it from the time the girls were little. To have that potential tapped so early in Padmé's life was a gift, and Jobal knew her daughter wouldn't squander it.

Ruwee met her in the living room, and she reached out to brush the last of the sawdust from his clothes. She wrinkled her nose as a fine cloud filled the air, not because she didn't like it, but because it always made her want to sneeze. Her husband leaned over and kissed her.

"Stop that," she said.

"It's a holiday!" he said. He had decided not to sulk about it, she guessed, and she appreciated that.

"You can celebrate later." She held out his hat and steered him into the foyer after he took hold of it.

She sat down to fasten her shoes and made sure he was putting on something other than his gardening clogs.

"Are you ready?" she asked.

"For our daughter to be Queen of Naboo?" he said.

He was quiet for a long moment, one hand resting on the door without opening it.

"You know, I think I am," he said. "I wasn't until right now, but she's worked so hard and I respect that."

"I wonder who she got her work ethic from," Jobal said,

rhetorically for the most part, but Ruwee never let anything slide.

"Are you saying it's our fault?" he asked.

"We had her offworld working on aid missions when she was seven," Jobal pointed out. "I just feel that might have contributed to her calling."

"I suppose you're right, my love," he said.

He offered his arm, and she took it. Together, they stepped out into the courtyard and joined their neighbors on the way to the polls.

Sheev Palpatine read over the taxation bill for the last time. Officially, it was the first time he'd seen it, and so he took care to make it look like he was reading deeply into the document. The truth was that he was preoccupied with several other things and was only checking the bill to make sure none of the details he required had been left out.

He would vote against it, of course. The bill would be a disaster for Naboo and for several other Mid Rim systems. And this time, at least, the bill wouldn't pass. He'd added enough matters of substance that the Trade Federation wouldn't be able to swallow to ensure that their allies would vote it down. But it would be another step closer. And he had the next three bills written, in any case.

"Senator, it's time," said one of his aides.

Palpatine let them herd him toward the Senate chambers, nodding at all the right people as they crossed paths in the corridors on the way to their pods. His face was bland, politely interested in what was being said around him. It was not an uncommon expression in the Senate hallways, but Palpatine had perfected it a long time ago. Soon enough, he would step into the spotlight and his colleagues would see that blandness drop away, but that would also be an act. No one ever saw his true face, the pure anger that burned in him.

But they might, someday.

𐌰𐌹𐌹𐌹

Padmé Naberrie had done the last thing she could. She had voted for herself when the candidates cast their ballots. She was sure each of them had, but for her, at least, it was the final step in proving to herself that she was ready. She trusted herself enough to be queen. The arrogance of it—thinking she was that much better than her fellows—rankled her a little bit, but Naboo had a failsafe in place for that.

She wouldn't rule as Padmé if she won. No one would even know who Padmé was, if everything went to plan. She would bear the robes and responsibilities of Naboo's crown, and she would give herself to that entirely, even to the extent of forsaking her own name for the duration of her reign. It was tradition, but it was a comfort, too—a reminder that her part was bigger than herself, that she would be acting in service, not selfishly for her own gain.

She hadn't really understood it until that morning, when her ballot-chip slid into the box. She thought the anonymity was for her protection, and in a way it was, but it was also to protect someone else. And it was time. *Her* time.

Amidala.

CHAPTER 2

The newly appointed Royal Guard gathered to hear the election results in the barracks. They came from all ranks and placements within the Security Forces and had been chosen to protect the new monarch, whoever she might be, because of their particular loyalty and dedication. Most of them knew each other already since the force wasn't very large, but this was the first time they had ever all been assembled in the same place, and these were their last few moments to relax before their new task began.

Panaka did not relax.

Just down the hall, the candidates were waiting for the results as well. They had been sequestered since that morning, each given their own small room in which to spend the day reflecting, and soon it would be Panaka's job to fetch the new queen. He knew which door he hoped to open, and was doing his best to pretend that he was still neutral, even though he was well past that point.

At last, the holonews switched over from the same pre-recorded election filler they had been running for the past hour and showed Governor Bibble. The silver-bearded governor was dressed in his usual purple, with a wide-sleeved overtunic that followed his every gesticulation with considerable vigor. A hush fell over the guards as Bibble cleared his throat and began the announcements.

"Citizens of Naboo," he began. Bibble always spoke as though performing for an audience, which made sense given his background in argumentative philosophy, and which he usually was, so it didn't seem too pompous. "I am pleased to inform you that after a well-fought race on the part of everyone, you have elected Candidate Amidala as your queen."

Bibble continued to speak as images of the candidate, now queen, flashed up, reminding anyone who might have forgotten about Amidala's age and campaign goals, but the guards were no longer listening. Every face in the room swiveled to Panaka, whose tightly clenched fists were the only outward sign of his emotions.

"Ready yourselves for inspection," he said, and then turned smartly on his heel to stride down the corridor to where the candidates were waiting.

It was traditional for the new queen to be greeted by her guard captain, a relic of Naboo's past, when candidates couldn't even be housed near one another or trust the legislature. Those days were long over, of course, but the Naboo encouraged remembrance over reenactment, and this was one of many steps taken to remind them how far they had come—and how far they had to go. She would meet Bibble as queen once she had inspected her personal guard.

Panaka paused for a moment outside Amidala's door, aware that everything was about to change. No longer was he just a guard captain, any more than she was just a candidate. He had liked her well enough during the campaign, but now their names would be linked forever in Naboo's history. It was worth taking a moment to reflect. Panaka waited a few moments longer while the election proctors readied themselves to tell the unsuccessful candidates, and then he opened the door.

"Your Highness," he said, standing on the threshold. "The election is over. Your work has begun."

Across the room, a slight figure rose to greet him. She was wearing a white dress that made her seem even younger than he knew she was, but he couldn't for a moment doubt the conviction in her stance. On the campaign trail, she had always been heavily made up, her face painted with cosmetics that reminded people of the weight of her promises. Now her face was bare, but with her hair down, it still wasn't easy to get a good look at her.

"Thank you, Captain," she said. "I am ready."

She gave nothing away, though Panaka imagined she must be at least a little bit nervous. He looked over his shoulder and saw the last of the proctors disappearing from the hall.

"If you will come with me?" he said, gesturing out of the

room. The droid floated off. "Your security team is ready for their inspection. A formality, as you know, but it's expected before Governor Bibble gets here to brief you officially."

"Of course, Captain," she said. Her voice was light and impersonal, but he was not offended. She barely knew him.

"Later we'll talk about how to personalize your security," Panaka said. "I have set up a few measures, but I didn't want to get too far ahead of you. It will take us a few days to get settled in, but I am very pleased with the team that has been assembled for you."

She didn't reply, but allowed him to lead her down the hall to where her guards were waiting. They stood in two lines and straightened to attention with no word from him as soon as he and the Queen came into the room. This was the Queen's personal guard, comprising sixteen guards who would protect her on a four-person rotation. The other palace guards could then concern themselves with operations and coordinate with the Queen as necessary. Panaka had wanted more personnel but had been overruled.

The Queen looked each guard in the face as they were introduced to her, committing names to memory. It should have been difficult to think of her as powerful just then, surrounded by people who were all so much bigger than she was, but she might have been three meters tall for how she carried herself. Once she was fully done up in the royal wardrobe, she would be exceptional.

When they reached the end of the line, Panaka dismissed all the guards except for the three who were on duty with him. The governor was shown in shortly after that. The early meetings did not take place in the throne room, and Panaka split his focus between watching the Queen and watching everyone else watch her. Bibble spoke mostly of procedure and rules, not of policy and substance, so it wasn't a particularly interesting conversation, but the Queen gave him her full attention.

"And that's really all we can cover today, I believe," Bibble wound up. It had been several hours, but the Queen showed no sign of exhaustion or boredom. "Unless you have any questions?"

"No, thank you, Governor Bibble," Queen Amidala said. Her inflection made it clear that it was a dismissal, even though technically Bibble still outranked her. Panaka smiled. "Though I would appreciate it if you could arrange for someone to send me any relevant political documents. I can read them tonight and be prepared for tomorrow's meetings."

"Of course, Your Highness," Bibble said, getting to his feet. He nodded to an aide, who made a note. "I shall send you the files as soon as I have finished the rest of my duties for today. It's a busy one for all of us."

The Queen nodded graciously to him, and the governor and his aides retired. Amidala got to her feet. Only now, with just the guards for company, did her bearing change. She stretched and rolled her neck, shaking her head like she was trying to resettle all the information she'd just acquired.

The transfer of power wouldn't happen for a few more days, and her first public appearances would follow shortly after. Despite the formal nature of the Queen's role and the relative rigidity of the protocols surrounding her, Naboo elections were not overly publicized. Once the candidates were sequestered for the voting, they didn't speak to the public until their full royal persona was ready.

"Captain?" she said, and the moment was over.

"Yes, Your Highness?" He came to stand in front of her.

"Would it be appropriate to discuss security over dinner?" she asked.

"There are supposed to be four of us on duty, Your Highness," Panaka said. "That means no eating for us, but I can still talk to you while you eat."

She sighed, but accepted the restriction. Panaka commed the kitchen and requested that a droid be sent up with dinner for one. Eventually, when they moved into the palace quarters, the Queen would be surrounded by people, but right now it was safer and easier to use droids.

"I'm not really used to eating by myself," she admitted as she sat down at the table. "My father knew we were all busy, but he liked it when we were together at meals."

She was being deliberately vague, he knew, even though he

was aware of her real identity. Panaka took that as a good sign. Some monarchs had played fast and loose with the anonymity their role required of them, and it was always a headache for their guards when they did. He hadn't been in the personal guard of the current queen, Sanandrassa, but he'd heard enough barracks gossip to know that her guards were looking forward to the day when she returned to having only one identity. It had always been something of a fight to separate her from her private persona. Panaka got the impression that his charge picked her battles much more carefully.

"That's one of the things I was hoping to speak to you about, Your Highness," Panaka said. If he felt awkward talking to her while she ate, he gave no indication.

"Oh?" she said, tearing her bread into small pieces.

"A queen traditionally has at least one handmaiden, as you know," he said. "I wondered if you had given any thought to yours."

"My sister has informed me she has no wish to serve in my government," the Queen said. "Which didn't surprise me at all. I have a few other friends I could request, I suppose, but I was very focused on the election. I didn't let myself imagine the practicalities that could follow."

"There's a girl at the Theed Conservatory," Panaka said. "She's your age and a decent musician. She's also very intelligent, and her instructors say she is levelheaded. I interviewed her a few weeks ago, just in case, and she seemed approachable."

The Queen raised an eyebrow, but did him the courtesy of not asking if he'd interviewed handmaidens on behalf of the other candidates, too.

"More importantly," he continued, "she bears a striking resemblance to you. If she was your handmaiden, and if she was interested, she could train as a bodyguard who would be closer to you than anyone else."

The Queen chewed thoughtfully and then took a drink of water.

"Is there a need for so much security?" she asked.

Queen Sanandrassa had focused on Naboo politics to the extreme of ignoring the rest of the sector, which made the other planets uncomfortable. Having two single-term queens in a row made *Panaka* uncomfortable. There were wider implications, too. Naboo had been dedicated to the election for the past month, but reports about Mid-Rim trade disputes had still made it to the front of the news.

"I believe in being prepared, Your Highness," Panaka said. "In an emergency, she could even switch places with you."

"I don't want to put another person in danger," the Queen said.

Before Panaka could give the obvious answer, her expression shifted, and he changed his mind. It was good that he could already understand her so well.

"It's unavoidable," she said. "That is who I am now."

"Yes, Your Highness," Panaka said. "We call it the burden of command, and nobody really likes it."

She paused again, turning the matter over while he watched. He saw her accept his premise, and then her expression immediately clouded again as she found another fault.

"What good would having one body double do?" the Queen said.

"Well, people would think she was you," Panaka explained. He thought they had cleared that.

"But if there are just two of us, and we switch, everyone will know," the Queen pointed out. "And if 'the Queen' is suddenly alone, people might be suspicious."

It hung there for a moment between them. Panaka was smart enough to realize that this was his first test. She had shown him up, and his response would influence how they interacted from this point forward. He swallowed his pride.

"That is a valid point, Your Highness," he said. "Do you have a suggestion?"

"If there are more than two of us, it will be much harder to tell," she said. "Not to mention, it will give you a way to ensure I have more than four guards on duty."

Oh, she was good.

"I will see what I can do," Panaka said. "It may take me a while to find suitable girls."

"Thank you, Captain," the Queen said. "I would like to

meet the girl you've already spoken to as soon as possible, if you can make the arrangements."

The Queen's personal comm device, which she had placed on the table while she ate, chimed.

"That's the governor," she said, checking it quickly. "I think that will be all for tonight, Captain."

"Your Highness," he said. "The guards will be stationed outside your door for the night."

The Queen took her plate and utensils to the droid that had delivered her dinner, then turned to go into the room where she would sleep the next few nights. Panaka moved to direct the guards into position.

"Oh," she said. "Captain, before I start reading, is there a secure way to contact my parents?"

"Your personal comm is completely secure, Your Highness," Panaka said. "It can be used to contact anyone on Naboo without a trace."

"Good night, Captain," the Queen said, and shut the door.

Panaka could tell the other guards were itching to gossip, but that would wait until they were off duty. He respected their job too much to let them cackle about it in the hallways. The others followed his example and stood quietly. They had only a bit of time before the new shift began, in any case.

Through the door, Panaka could hear the Queen speaking, presumably to her parents. Her voice was too low to make out any of the words, but he could hear the rise and fall of her tone as she spoke to them. She was a challenge to read. Most fourteen-year-olds, even the brilliant ones, showed some emotions when they spoke, but the Queen had hardly done that all afternoon. Even her response to her election had been cold.

The replacement guards showed up on schedule, and Panaka headed back to the rooms he shared with Mariek. He looked forward to sharing his impressions of their new monarch, and asking for his wife's input after she had met her as well. About halfway home, he realized that while he had no idea what was going on in Amidala's head, he hadn't once, in the entire course of the afternoon, forgotten she was the Queen.

CHAPTER 3

For the first time since Captain Panaka had opened the door to tell her the election results, Padmé let herself relax. It had been a long afternoon—the first of many, she was sure—and though she wasn't exactly tired, she was tired of holding her face so still. She had decided early on in the campaign that she was going to present herself as the stoic, measured option. Her actions would be enough to show her compassion without having to write it all over her face. Though it got easier every day, such control did not yet come naturally to her, and sometimes she just wanted to *smile*.

She lay back on the bed, a grin stretching across her face. She had *done* it. The months of planning and preparation, of training herself to look a certain way no matter how she felt, of isolating herself from her family and friends, had worked, and she was Queen of Naboo. She groped for a pillow and put it over her mouth, smothering the giggle that boiled up out of her. The guards were, after all, right outside her door, and Padmé hadn't yet decided if Amidala was the type who giggled, even in private.

She let herself bask in the feeling for several minutes

before she sat up and got back to work. From what she could tell, Bibble had sent every document the planetary government had produced in the past few months, and even though she was aware of most of the issues, this would be her first access to the privy details. She couldn't wait to get to them. But first, there was something she had to do.

She held her private comm in her hand and called her parents. She hoped she hadn't kept them waiting too long. They had been quite understanding of her ambitions, even if her father didn't entirely think it was a good idea, and hopefully they would know why she hadn't been able to call them earlier in the day.

"Congratulations!" Jobal's voice came through the connection with pristine clarity as she stepped into the projection.

"Thanks, Mom," Padmé said. She let herself smile again. She could always be herself with her parents.

"We're so proud of you," Ruwee added, appearing beside his wife.

Coming from her father, those words meant more than Padmé could say. She knew he understood that, and that her smile would always be enough for him, queen or not.

"I'm sorry I couldn't call and tell you myself," Padmé said. "It's been a very busy day."

"I can imagine," Ruwee said with a laugh. "Sio lives for this sort of thing."

Having a father who was known at least by reputation to

most of the important people on the planet had never really impacted Padmé's life. Ruwee had the gift of knowing how to be friends with powerful people without taking advantage of it, and it was something Padmé admired about him. He very rarely slipped up, but she supposed this was an exciting day for him, too.

"Anyway," Ruwee continued, "we both understand that your time is going to be spoken for a lot. We've known that since you entered the campaign. Politics moves your priorities around, and we trust you enough to make those decisions."

"What your father is trying to say," Jobal said, jumping in, "is that we know you're busy and excited, and we're going to hear about you on the holonews, and we love you anyway."

"That is not at all what I was trying to say," Ruwee said.

Padmé laughed. She kept it quiet, but didn't raise her hand to muffle the sound. Her mother had always encouraged her dreams as much as her father had tempered them with practicalities. They were two different approaches to the same destination and, Padmé had learned, two different ways to show love.

"I'll remember who I am, Dad," Padmé said. "No matter who I'm talking to or what I have to look like."

"That's all I wanted to hear," Ruwee said.

"I wanted to hear about your rooms, but I guess you don't have those yet," Jobal said. The private apartments in Theed's palace were very, very rarely open to the public. For security, and other reasons, little was known about their appearance, but there were rumors that they held some truly great pieces of art, and Jobal was highly interested in that sort of thing.

"Not for a couple more days," Padmé said. "I'm in the palace now, but not the royal part yet. Queen Sanandrassa is probably packing up, but the official transfer of power isn't until the end of the week."

From her study of the blueprints, Padmé was reasonably sure that her current room was a few floors directly below the royal apartment, but she assumed the upper floors were laid out differently. Eventually, her guards and staff would live where she was staying now.

She heard a chime through the comlink, and both of her parents looked away for a moment.

"Sorry, your father is hosting his usual postelection get-together," Jobal said as Ruwee disappeared from the frame.

"That's all right," Padmé said. "I still have a lot to do."

Mother and daughter lapsed into comfortable silence while they waited for Ruwee to come back.

"Give my love to Sola," Padmé said as Ruwee returned to the frame.

Her parents said good night, and she turned off the comm. She thought of her parents' house tonight, full of friends celebrating and theorizing what was going to come next. For a moment, she was painfully lonely. And then it struck her: she was going to be what everyone was talking about. Yes, there were new representatives in the legislature to discuss, too, but the primary focus of most conversations tonight would be the new Queen of Naboo, and that was *her*.

It was an incredible responsibility. And Padmé was so, so excited.

ア∀∀⅄

Coruscant was, at times, made of light. It shone like a beacon—the seat of the great Republic Senate, attracting attention from systems in every corner of the galaxy. Like mynocks to a transistor coupling, all kinds of people were drawn to the power of the city-planet, and all of them basked in the glow.

But Coruscant was also full of structures and cables and the detritus of centuries of continuous habitation, and in the shadows of those things, there was always plenty of space for the dark. In the seedy corners of the undercity, cruelty festered, and looked for places to grow.

Darth Sidious rarely bothered with the lower levels. He had ways to exploit them if he wanted something, of course, but it was far more his style to bring darkness into places where people thought they were beyond its reach. He found the weak points, the cracks where the light got out, and shoved the darkness in. He played a long game, a smart game, and unfortunately, from time to time, that meant dealing with people who failed to understand the grand scope of his vision.

Despite his personal distaste for them, the lower levels were a good place to have a discreet conversation. Sidious rarely bothered with having those in person either, but he knew that his presence could be overwhelming and he had no issue pressing that advantage when one of his so-called allies was faltering.

Nute Gunray had been ranting for several minutes about the failed bill. Sidious had more or less been ignoring him the whole time. It wasn't important. At the end of the day, Gunray himself wasn't all that important. Useful, yes, particularly given his suggestibility and willingness to spend vast amounts of money on a disposable fighting force, but not important.

"And then that senator from Naboo insisted on the bypass amendment, and it cost us the entire Delcontrian faction," Gunray wound up. "We did everything we could, but the votes were against us."

"It doesn't matter," Sidious snapped. He had learned a great deal from this failed bill. How far Malastare was willing to go. How much the Tellonites were willing to lose. Whom the Caladarians were willing to sacrifice. "You will have a new bill in the next few days."

"Dodd won't be able to introduce it," Gunray said. "It's too obvious."

"Of course it is," Sidious said. He was surrounded by idiots. "Someone from the Delcontrian faction will introduce it."

"But we just lost them!" Gunray protested.

"That was Naboo's fault," Sidious said. "This new bill will win them back."

Gunray muttered something too quietly for Sidious to hear, and then immediately looked fearful. Under the cowl of his hood, Sidious smiled. They needed him so badly, for their petty little squabbles, and he terrified them completely. It was one of his chief delights.

"Someone will contact you," Sidious continued as though nothing had happened.

"Yes, my lord," Gunray said. He bowed obsequiously, and Sidious cut the connection before he could say anything else.

The Neimoidians were troublesome. It was always a challenge to find someone just incompetent enough, and while Sidious enjoyed the thrill of it, sometimes it required more of his supervision than he liked to give. He needed agents who could act independently, but it wasn't time for them yet. There were too many pieces, too many outcomes, to let someone who could think for themselves start messing around.

Still, there was never any harm in being prepared. Sidious changed comm channels and reached out to his apprentice.

Amidala had won. Tsabin watched the announcement, along with everyone else on the planet, and felt something unfurl in her chest she'd never felt before. This was what success felt like, even if it wasn't precisely hers yet. She left the room where the other students were watching the full results and went back to her small quarters.

Queen Amidala. It sounded regal. Perfect. Beautiful. And, to all appearances, the Queen herself was all three. She must be brilliant as well, but Tsabin knew that brilliance alone wasn't enough to run a planet. Charm, that elusive quality Tsabin had never possessed, was a part of it, too.

She pulled her carry case out from under her bed and opened it. The bag was a bit dusty, but aside from that, it was empty and ready to go. She turned to her desk, where three acceptance letters were stacked. Pretentiously written on arbovellum—real paper—they were offers to sit in the back row of three different orchestras. She hadn't read any of them past the first few lines. Now, she swept them into the garbage disposal and gathered up what knickknacks had accumulated on her desk. These went into her carry case, along with her spare clothes and the other belongings she'd brought with her to the conservatory.

Last, she pulled down her hallikset case. She opened it up and looked at the instrument that was the cause of so much of her stress and joy. Her fingers brushed the silent strings. But her decision was already made.

Tsabin shut the case and placed it on top of her larger one. Then she sat down on her bed to wait, reading through the election results on her personal screen. There were no great surprises this year. Only an odd fluttering in her chest that something was finally going to go right for *her*.

And when Captain Panaka came back, Tsabin would absolutely be ready to go.

CHAPTER 4

In hindsight, perhaps she should not have met Tsabin for the first time as the Queen. It had made perfect sense at the time. Padmé had several meetings in the morning with various officials and palace employees, and when Panaka announced it was time for the final meeting of the afternoon, Padmé hadn't slipped out of her role. So Tsabin had met her as a cool and distant monarch, and not as someone who was going to get to know her like a second skin.

To her credit, Padmé realized the error almost as soon as Panaka was finished introducing the girls to each other.

"Thank you, Captain," Amidala said. "That will be all for now."

Panaka was surprised to be dismissed; he wouldn't be on duty again until the next day, but he'd swallowed any protests he might have made and left them to it. Then the two of them were staring at each other in an awkward silence. Padmé's eyes flicked to the guards, who were pretending not to be there. She didn't have a complete read on them yet, so she wasn't sure how far their discretion would go. They never accompanied her into the room where she slept, though. And there were two chairs in there, she remembered.

"Walk with me?" she said, getting to her feet and holding out an arm.

Tsabin nodded and fell into step beside her. Padmé led the way into the bedroom and shut the door behind them.

"This is more complicated than I was imagining," she said. "Please, sit down."

Tsabin did as she was told. So far, as a matter of fact, she had been entirely biddable, and her face hadn't shown any emotion. Padmé could completely understand that.

"Royal handmaidens are traditionally attached to a queen to serve in her private household," Padmé said as a place to start. "I don't know if Captain Panaka has told you the same things that he's told me, but that is not exactly what I'm looking for."

"The captain said you are looking for a bodyguard, but not the usual kind," Tsabin said. "I wouldn't be defending you with a blaster. I'd be defending you with my identity."

"No monarch has had a bodyguard like that since the last dispute with the Gungans, and that was generations ago," Padmé said. "And I am still not entirely sure that there is a reason to return to the practice."

"My impression of Captain Panaka is that he is more of a 'no reason *not* to' sort of thinker," Tsabin said.

She was still sitting stiffly in the chair. Padmé slouched in her own seat, and watched with some satisfaction as Tsabin's shoulders relaxed.

"I agree," Padmé said. "I don't think there's any harm in following his advice."

"Or," Tsabin suggested, a hint of mischief in her voice for the first time, "letting him think that most of his advice is being followed."

Padmé didn't try to stop the smile that spread across her face. She was not a deceptive person by nature, but she did understand the value of keeping her cards close.

"My name is Padmé," she said. It was the greatest show of trust she could think of. And it was enough.

"I'm pleased to meet you," Tsabin said, finally looking at her with an unguarded expression.

Padmé leaned farther back into her chair. She kicked off her slippers and crossed her feet in front of her, her knees leaning on the armrests.

"I've already changed the captain's plan a little bit," she said. "He thought one bodyguard would be enough, but I have convinced him that a group is a better idea."

"Because it's easier to hide," Tsabin mused. "Do you know who?"

"Not yet," Padmé said. "We only talked about it yesterday. But he found you, and I assume he had other people in mind when he decided that you were the one to bring in."

"We should be loyal to you, not to him," Tsabin said

quickly. "They have me staying in the barracks with the other guards, and I don't think that's a good idea."

Padmé hadn't considered that.

"He recruited me because I am good at providing support. It's what I've always done for any group I've ever played with. But I don't think that's all I have to offer," Tsabin said. When Padmé said nothing, she continued, "Hallikset players spend years on breath control, even though it's a stringed instrument. It's part of the discipline, but also helps maintain the purity of the sound. I can breathe without anyone noticing, and that means I can control my face and my reactions."

"I wondered how you did it," Padmé said. "You're very good."

"I can teach you," Tsabin said immediately. This was going to be more fun than Padmé had thought. "It's possible that we'll have different gut reactions to things, but if we both learn the same way of concealing those reactions, no one will be able to tell."

They talked for a while longer about themselves, getting to know each other. A droid brought dinner, and the sun went down, and neither girl particularly cared. Tsabin was quick to understand Padmé's ideas, and quicker still to provide suggestions to improve them. The plan was by no means perfect, but it was a good start.

"That's probably as much as we can do before the others

get here," Padmé said. "It wouldn't make any sense to set up the whole stage before we have all the players on it."

"I can show you the breathing exercises, at least," Tsabin said.

"Let me call a droid first," Padmé said, making the decision for them both. "You're not staying in the barracks."

⟆⩒⩒⩒⩒

The room Tsabin had stayed in at the conservatory was small, but it was all her own. She'd never shared a room with another person before, and Padmé hadn't asked. Tsabin quickly buried her resentment. She didn't want to stay in the barracks anyway, and she was going to have to get used to following Padmé's orders. Or, rather, Amidala's orders. It was an ongoing challenge to tell them apart, but also: that was part of her job.

Tsabin's things arrived just as they finished the second set of exercises. The guard who knocked on the door kept her face carefully bland, and Tsabin could imagine the report that would be submitted at the end of the shift. She decided she didn't care.

They would be moving into the royal apartments soon enough, so Tsabin didn't bother to fully unpack. She got her pajamas and followed Padmé's directions to the refresher. It was much nicer than the one at the conservatory.

"I'm still working on figuring it out," Padmé said, after they had gone to bed. "The differences between Padmé and Amidala, I mean. I think with you I'll have to be both."

It was not quite an apology, but Tsabin understood.

"I promise to wait until after your reign is over before I write a tell-all for the holos about all the things you messed up in the early days," she said.

Padmé laughed.

"I think the Queen and her new handmaiden are up to something," Panaka said.

He picked at his dinner, or whatever you called the meal you brought your wife in the middle of the night when she was on a break from work and you hadn't seen each other properly in a few days. The palace was quiet at night, but Mariek took her duties seriously and wouldn't stray too far from the diplomatic wing, even though it was currently unoccupied.

"They're teenage girls," Mariek said. "They are always going to be up to something."

"How can I protect her if I don't know what she's doing?" he asked.

"Protect her from what, exactly?" Mariek said. "I know you like to be prepared for things, but this feels excessive, even for you."

Panaka put his chopsticks down.

"If there are problems with commerce in the Mid Rim, Naboo will be swept right along into it," he said.

"That's why we have a senator," Mariek told him. "A senator you like, you'll remember, and who is actually friends with you for some reason."

Mariek and Palpatine politely tolerated each other, but neither could see what Panaka saw in the other.

"I am a very likable person," Panaka said. "Just ask anyone."

"You did bring me dinner," Mariek allowed. "Twice, since you're not going to eat yours, apparently."

He handed over his plate so she could keep stealing things from it without reaching across the little table in the break room.

Obi-Wan Kenobi did not like politicians. It was nothing personal. To be honest, he didn't *know* that many politicians, and those he did know were generally decent to him, even though he was only a Padawan. The problem was that politicians wrote so many things down, and then Obi-Wan had to read them, because his master had a *feeling* that something was coming. Qui-Gon had a deeply annoying habit of being correct about this sort of thing, which was one of the reasons Obi-Wan hadn't mutinied. Well, that and because he'd tried something very like mutiny once, and it hadn't gone well.

He was a Jedi apprentice. He was supposed to be meditating on his lightsaber forms. Or helping his peers contemplate their feelings. Or rearranging stones in the rock garden. Or doing *literally anything* else, but no: he was reading Senate bills about tax reforms for space lanes that went to planets he'd never heard of. At least he'd always liked the library in the Jedi Temple. Jocasta was friendly to Qui-Gon and didn't seem to mind his odd requests even though she bucked when anyone else asked for her assistance. And it was quiet. Sometimes Obi-Wan was just really, really grateful for the quiet.

"What do you think, Obi-Wan?" Qui-Gon asked. He didn't look up from the file he was reading. Obi-Wan resisted the urge to squirm.

Having a master who could sense your discontent was a real pain sometimes. It had averted disaster on a couple of occasions, but it was still embarrassing. Obi-Wan had hoped to leave it behind in his childhood, but he'd settle for cutting it off with his braid when the time came.

"I think there are a great many people who have too much time on their hands," Obi-Wan said. He leaned back in his chair and rubbed his face. "And I think I don't understand why it's so important that they spend that time talking about this."

"It's a matter of perspective, my young apprentice," Qui-Gon admonished him. He looked up from the file and gave

Obi-Wan his full attention. "The most important thing to the people who do this is control."

"The Jedi think control is important, too." Obi-Wan slid into the argument with the ease of long practice. Sometimes he and his master argued when they didn't even disagree.

"A Jedi controls themself," Qui-Gon said, which was more or less what Obi-Wan was anticipating. The familiar back-and-forth was a hard-won rhythm, and for all his personal misgivings, Obi-Wan wouldn't have given it up for anything.

"Politicians seek to control others," Obi-Wan said.

"It's not just politicians, but yes," Qui-Gon said. "These taxes would drive a wedge between planets and the corporations they trade with. That's a lot of control to lose."

"And what are *we* doing, Master?" Obi-Wan asked. He was used to Qui-Gon getting involved in things the Council didn't entirely approve of, but he appreciated some advance warning about when it was going to happen, if only so he could pack.

"We are listening, Obi-Wan," Qui-Gon said. "So that when the time comes, we will be able to act."

"With or without orders?" Obi-Wan asked.

Qui-Gon smiled indulgently. It would have bothered Obi-Wan, once upon a time. As a boy he'd held the Council in such high regard, the be-all and end-all of true Jedi ambition. He still didn't entirely agree with Qui-Gon's approach to things, but he had long ago accepted it as a viable alternative. It was, after all, important to avoid absolutes.

"I think we'll be more or less in alignment with the Council this time, my young Padawan. You don't have to start worrying yet."

"At least that means we'll be less likely to get involved in local labor disputes," Obi-Wan said.

"Or kick-start unlikely romances with the local nobility." The rebuke in Qui-Gon's tone for Obi-Wan's choice of wording was unmistakable: some things were too serious to be understated.

Obi-Wan coughed, and changed the subject.

In a factory on Geonosis, a very large order was registered in the central computer. The furnaces flared under the desert sun, and a river of molten metal began its journey. The production line clanked to life.

CHAPTER 5

At the end of the week, Queen Amidala appeared on the steps of Theed palace. For the first time, she was dressed for the part. Her dress was red with a wide, ruffled skirt. The bodice was stitched with gold thread, and the wide sleeves were lined with gold fabric, turned back against her elbow so that the color shone in the sun. She wore the headpiece that she had worn as a candidate. It was less dramatic than the one the soon-to-be-former Queen Sanandrassa was wearing, but it was still marked by elaborate braids and curls. Tsabin had pinned it on that morning, and Padmé had remarked it was much easier for Tsabin to reach the back of her head. Tsabin had also done Padmé's makeup, painting on the royal symbols for the first time.

It was pageantry, but it was necessary. A planetwide invitation had been issued for the coronation, and all of the schools and academies had been given a holiday. Amidala was the youngest queen in quite some time, and her Ascendancy was to be a spectacle, even by Naboo standards. The girls had left nothing to chance. Even Tsabin's robes, dyed the same color as Padmé's dress, had been selected to make her as unremarkable as possible. She had followed in the procession, and it was entirely possible that no one saw her, even as she stood next to Amidala on the steps. Panaka led a contingent of guards behind, but today they were entirely ceremonial, and arranged themselves in loose formation.

Sanandrassa stood beside Padmé at the top of the palace stairs, carrying the symbols of the Naboo monarch. Governor Bibble stepped between the two women and accepted the scepter into his hands. For that brief moment, Naboo had no queen at all. Then Bibble turned to Amidala and held out the scepter. She picked it up with both hands and held it high for the assembled crowd to see. Bibble smiled broadly as the plaza filled with cheers and flower petals, and both queens looked out over the people with solemn expressions.

Sanandrassa led the way through the palace doors when the ceremony was done. Padmé walked beside her. She had been in the palace on school trips, but never on such a momentous day, and this was the first time she'd met the Queen as an equal, not a candidate. Sanandrassa pointed out various artwork as they went along so that Padmé could gawk in a polite way.

"You may select your own pieces, of course," Sanandrassa said. "Especially if there are artists you are interested in."

"It all looks magnificent," Amidala said. "Changing a single piece would ruin the effect."

"Perhaps," Sanandrassa said. "But keep the idea in mind. Sometimes your control of your surroundings is all you have."

Padmé never, ever intended to be pushed that far. Still, a bit more blue might be nice. And there was a girl in the southern province who was doing amazing work with water sculptures.

They reached the throne room at last, and Sanandrassa paused on the threshold to let Padmé enjoy the moment. The room was large and round, with the seats arranged in a circle under the broad dome of the roof. It was an arrangement for conversations, not audiences, which was the preferred style of Naboo governance. But there could be no doubt about which chair was Amidala's.

Padmé straightened her spine and walked across the floor to the throne. The actual chair was strangely narrow, and pitched forward so that she would always appear to be taller than she was. Careful of her skirt, she stepped up onto the platform in front of the chair, turned as gracefully as possible, and leaned into the seat. Her skirt collapsed under her as she sat on it, the bustle folding in on itself so that it didn't impede her posture. She placed one hand on each of the throne's armrests and looked into Sanandrassa's face.

"Your Highness," the former queen said.

Then she took one of the other seats. The government officials sat down once the Queen was settled, and the guards—including Tsabin—disappeared into the wall decorations.

"Thank you," Amidala said. "We are hopeful that we will fill this role as well as you have."

The governor took over the conversation at that point, and Padmé let him. There was no real work to be done today by any member of the government besides him. Padmé watched the faces of the other officials, memorizing their names and faces even as she learned the sort of expressions they made as they reacted to what was said. None of them had even a fraction of the control Tsabin was teaching her, but members of the legislature ran under their own names and reputations, so they didn't really require it.

An aide approached Panaka and whispered in his ear.

"Your Highness," Panaka said, interrupting Sanandrassa's description of the school for weavers she planned to found. "My apologies, but there is an incoming transmission from Senator Palpatine."

"Of course, Captain," Amidala said, and Panaka activated the holoemitters in the middle of the throne room floor.

Palpatine was dressed in his traditional wide-sleeved tunic, even though Panaka was reasonably sure it was the middle of the night on Coruscant.

"Queen Amidala," Palpatine said, bowing slightly. "Allow me to offer my congratulations. I won't keep you long, but I wanted to convey my greetings to you personally."

"Senator Palpatine," Amidala said, nodding in acknowledgment. She stayed as cool and formal as she could. "We look forward to working with you on behalf of Naboo and its people."

"As do I," Palpatine said. He turned to Sanandrassa. "My lady, it has been my pleasure."

"Thank you, Senator," Sanandrassa said. There was no way to tell what they really thought about each other.

The senator made his excuses and disappeared.

"On the rare occasions you have to deal with offworld issues, the senator is your best resource," Sanandrassa said. "He's very busy, of course, but he always has time to pay close attention to his home planet."

Padmé nodded politely. She had her own opinions about how Sanandrassa had dealt with offworld issues, but this was hardly the time to bring them into the conversation.

"In any case, Your Highness," Sanandrassa continued, "my effects were removed from the royal apartment this morning, and I am ready to depart at your leisure."

"Thank you for your welcome today," Padmé replied.

She wished that there were some ritual words she was supposed to say, some finite way of ending the conversation without dismissing Sanandrassa directly. Fortunately, the governor chimed in with his own farewells and offered to see the ex-monarch to her conveyance, and that took care of two problems at once.

At last it was just Padmé, Tsabin, and the guards in the throne room. Padmé took advantage of the relative privacy to give herself another moment to bask in her victory. Subtly, of course. She drank in the beauty of the room, the carved wooden chairs and the delicate marble. These trappings were not the most important aspect of her new job, but Padmé was Naboo to her fingertips: she knew how to appreciate good art, and the throne room was full of it.

"Captain Panaka," she said, reining in her wayward emotions, "would you see us up to the royal apartment?"

Panaka had every intention of conducting his own inspection of the suite, and Padmé allowed him the space to do it while she and Tsabin unpacked their few personal belongings in the largest bedroom. The suite consisted of a dressing room, a sitting room, a small meeting room, and three rooms for sleeping, one of which was obviously intended for the Queen. There was also an extensive wardrobe system attached to the dressing room, but it was still being stocked and was not yet ready for examination.

"We may have to move some of the furniture in the sitting room," Panaka reported when his inspection was done. "There's no good place for your guards to stand."

"I don't need my guards in the room with me at all times, Captain," Padmé said. "That is why you wanted Tsabin here."

Panaka's face darkened under the brim of his hat as he fought to keep himself from a grimace.

"Your Highness, Tsabin is not meant to be your only guard in here," he said. "We can cut the rotation down to two guards in the room and the other two in the corridor, but—"

"No, Captain." It was the first time Amidala had truly brought her will to bear, and everyone flinched. She looked absolutely splendid in that dress, like a red-gold comet that was going to go exactly where it wanted. Panaka's stance shifted slightly to something defensive. "We are on the fifth floor. The only other people who live in this section of the palace are the guards you selected yourself. Any craft approaching the balcony would be spotted long before it got here. I thank you for your dedication, but I will not require any of your guards in my rooms."

It was the moment when they would all figure out how far the Queen could be pushed, and it was happening in front of several witnesses.

For a heartbeat or two, Tsabin thought there was going to be an argument. Panaka did not look like he was going to back down, and she knew there was no way Padmé would.

"Very well, Your Highness." Panaka looked like he had swallowed a sourfruit. "Tsabin, we'll begin your combat training tomorrow."

"You'll teach us both," Padmé said firmly. "The others, too, when they arrive."

"Of course, Your Highness." Panaka didn't wait for her

dismissal. He turned on his heel and led the guards out of the room.

For a few moments after the door was shut, the girls stood there in silence.

"Do you really trust me that much already?" Tsabin asked. The sleeves of her robes hid her twisting fingers. It was the one part of her body she didn't control, because usually she had to move her fingers when she was performing anyway.

"No," Padmé said. She reached up and pulled the head-piece off. A few pins fell into her skirt, and she shook them to the floor so she could retrieve them. "But I am going to eventually, so we might as well establish boundaries at the start."

They went into the dressing room, and Tsabin helped Padmé into a set of robes that matched her own. Padmé brushed her hair out from the braids they'd put it in under the headpiece, and wiped her face clean. Tsabin opened the wardrobe door and fiddled with the controls for a moment until she figured out how to send the dress to its assigned spot.

"Why don't you like Sanandrassa?" Tsabin asked once they were back in the sitting room, reclining with their feet up on one of the footstools Panaka had wanted to move.

"Was it that obvious?" Padmé said. She sounded more concerned about that than anything else so far, but Tsabin knew it was only because the Queen let her guard down a bit when they were alone.

"Probably not," Tsabin told her. She linked her fingers in

her lap the way Padmé did. It wasn't just combat training they had to share. "I learn your tells as you learn to hide them, that's all."

"It's not that I dislike her as a person," Padmé said after considering it for a moment. "But I didn't like how she talked about the other planets in the sector during her reign. We share one senator, but she talked like Naboo was the only planet out here. I'd rather reach out and make allies. Naboo traditions are important, but they aren't the only things that matter in the galaxy."

"You didn't mention that on the campaign trail," Tsabin said.

"No," Padmé allowed. "But it's on my list."

"I imagine your list makes Captain Panaka quake in his boots," Tsabin said.

"Probably," Padmé said. "We'll break it to him gently."

"It's time for your breathing exercises, Your Highness," Tsabin said, and they got back to work.

Watching Padmé relax without actually relaxing was a bit unnerving, but Tsabin knew that most people would only see the studied calm of the Queen's face. Padmé had to work hardest at not showing her compassion in her eyes, so Tsabin had already modified their practice to focus on appearing politely interested, not placid. It was difficult for Tsabin, because she had done her best to train herself to disappear entirely, and now her role called for both. To be perfectly honest, she hadn't had this much fun in years, and she'd never felt so useful.

A few more deep breaths and Padmé had it, the face Amidala would wear in public. Tsabin blinked twice, flexed her fingers in her sleeves, and matched her exactly.

Their proud smiles were identical.

CUNNING

ᄂᄂᄉᄉᆻᄑ

"Did you know that there is—officially—no such thing as a jail on Naboo?" Panaka said artlessly. The girl across the table from him rolled her eyes.

"Only because we send everyone to the moon," she replied. She spoke in the carefully clipped tones of someone who was modulating their natural accent.

"Exactly," said Panaka. "Just so we're both clear where this is headed."

The second eye-roll was a smidgen less sure of itself.

Panaka had found Rabene Tonsort on a list of dropouts from one of Naboo's more prestigious schools. She was, according to her record, brilliant in a variety of media, from music to acting to sculpture. Her teachers praised her creativity and adaptability. Her classmates—she had few friends—enjoyed working with her, since she always seemed to deliver results. School administrators had thrown her out when it was discovered she'd been running a forgery ring out of the school's basement. Several other students had been suspected, but the only hard evidence anyone ever found pinned the entire operation on Rabene.

"You're a fairly accomplished conwoman, I see," Panaka continued. "Or is it congirl?"

Naboo children tended to be prodigies. It only made sense that some of them went in strange directions.

"It was a school project," Rabene protested, her accent slipping through the cracks of her emotional response. "We were supposed to conduct a survey of an artistic era of our choice. It's right on the syllabus."

"You were not supposed to sell the results," Panaka said. "And you certainly weren't supposed to tell the offworlders you sold them to that they were the original pieces."

Rabene said nothing.

"What I don't understand," Panaka continued, "is that you could clearly do whatever you want. An artist with your versatility comes along once a generation if we're lucky. You have the whole of Naboo at your fingertips, and you choose this."

There was no actual danger of Rabene being sent to the moon, but Panaka wasn't about to tell her that. The school, unwilling to admit it had fostered a criminal, had simply forced her to drop out. She hadn't even been expelled.

"Why not go legit and be an actress?" Panaka asked. Naboo went through trends, same as anywhere else, and the theater was currently the most popular.

"I don't like playing parts that other people have written," Rabene said. It might have even been the truth, so Panaka decided to roll with it.

"What if it was the part of a lifetime?" he said.

He tried to say it as casually as possible, leave as much up to her imagination as he could. She leaned forward immediately.

"I will not be an informant," she hissed.

Panaka laughed. A real, true laugh. That wasn't at all what he was talking about, and for some reason, her complete denial amused him. Too late, he realized that he was probably giving too much away, but honestly, it had been so long since he laughed like that he almost didn't care.

"I'm not asking you to be an informant," he said. "It actually has nothing to do with your previous indiscretions. You just have a few talents I'm interested in, and no other offers at the moment."

"I'm listening," she said.

Panaka had made all of his selections very carefully. One girl had been eliminated from consideration because she lacked the hand-eye coordination to fire a blaster. Several others were already too well-known in the Naboo arts community for them to disappear without it being remarked upon. Rabene might be a bit rough around the edges, but she was perfect otherwise, and Panaka didn't mind having something to hold over her in an emergency.

"It's a security job," Panaka said. "You'd be charged with protecting one person, and that protection would extend to performing duties around her household."

It was appropriately vague.

"Like laundry and cleaning?" Rabene asked.

"If the occasion called for it." Panaka had no real idea what Amidala was going to do with her handmaidens once she had them, though he doubted their tasks would be mundane.

"But it's very high profile," Rabene mused. "So high profile that you can't tell me who it is."

"Not until I have some indication of your trustworthiness or commitment," he admitted.

"Please, Captain," Rabene said. "You're a Royal Security officer. There aren't that many people it could be."

Panaka wondered absently how many times he was going to be outsmarted by a teenage girl in the days to come.

"All right," he said. "You have some idea of the stakes. You have some idea of the responsibility. I want you to do this because you are good at something she's not."

"Deceit," Rabene said.

"Precisely," Panaka said. "I want you to make the system work. To teach her how to hide in plain sight and how to blend into the wall decorations. I want you to watch for things she doesn't know how to watch for. I want you to teach her how to spot a fake, and how to talk to someone and make them trust her without relying on her compassionate heart."

"She's been elected queen," Rabene said. "There's no way she doesn't know how to do at least some of that already."

"That's as may be," Panaka said. "But I want you to make it part of her arsenal, not something she only falls back on as a last resort."

Rabene looked at him for a long moment. Panaka wasn't sure what she was looking for, but whatever it was, it was clear in her face the moment she found it. He had her. Whatever Amidala cooked up with the others, he would have one handmaiden whom he could rely on. It made him feel a bit tawdry—she was only a girl, after all—but this was planetary safety, and Panaka would leave nothing to chance. This was one thing he could control.

"Very well then, Captain Panaka. I'm in," she said. She smiled at him, all sweetness and light, and he wasn't fooled for an instant. "I'll teach your queen bee how to use her sting."

CHAPTER 6

There were five of them altogether, including Tsabin, who already stood behind the throne. Panaka presented them to the Queen with minimal flourish at the end of the second week of her reign. They each bowed politely when he put them forward, and Amidala acknowledged them with an identical nod. Her face was painted for full court, and her elaborate headpiece extended from her head in both directions. She was carefully impersonal, a mystery in voluminous green. Panaka was decently sure she hadn't actually moved in several hours, but there was no indication that her attention was flagging.

It had been a long day with the regional representatives—there was a projected labor shortage for this year's grain harvest, and debate was split over whether to bring in off-worlders to help with the work or to simply buy food from off planet and let the grain become next season's fertilizer—and they were all eager to wrap up. Still, Amidala sat straight-backed on her throne and looked each girl full in the face as Panaka introduced them.

"Rabene Tonsort, gifted artist and actress." Rabene's

placid expression indicated there was a great deal Panaka left out of her biography. "Eirtama Ballory, scientist and engineer; Suyan Higin, seamstress and maker; and Sashah Adova—"

Panaka trailed off as Sashah bowed, unable to quantify why exactly he thought the twelve-year-old was qualified for this, even though there was no doubt in his mind that she was. Amidala caught his pause and risked half a smile, more emotion than she usually showed in public.

"Thank you, Captain," she said, as though the introductions had been completed without incident. "You have done a remarkable job in a short time to find such excellent candidates."

"It is my privilege," Panaka said, bowing.

"We will go up to the suite and talk further," Amidala continued, now speaking directly to the girls. "There are a few things we need to discuss."

Panaka ground his teeth. Amidala had been exceptionally firm about not allowing guards into the suite without a very good reason, and he had a feeling she would shut him out of the coming conversation quite deliberately.

The Queen rose and led the way upstairs. The girls followed her into her rooms, and Tsabin shut the door, doing her best not to smile at Panaka's expression. In the sitting room, Amidala indicated that they should all sit down, and then she perched on a chair by the hearth and pulled her headpiece off. Tsabin was standing next to her before she'd finished extricating herself from all the pins, and accepted the handoff seamlessly.

"Just put it on the table for now," Amidala said. Tsabin did, and took her seat again.

Padmé took a moment to shake her hair out and look at the girls Panaka had chosen. They were all physically similar to her, except Eirtama, who was blonde, and they all looked politely interested. Even Sashah wasn't cowed by the apartment. Padmé was impressed.

"My name is Padmé," she said, by way of introduction. She wanted them to understand. "I imagine Captain Panaka has explained the dangerous aspects of this position well enough, but I am hoping for something else in addition to bodyguards."

"It's not an addition," Sashah said. She had a dreamy voice. "It's an expansion."

"Indeed," Padmé said. "But it's also a collaboration. Panaka selected each of you because you have talents that I do not. I want to take that beginning and make us into something even stronger."

"Not just six parts," Suyan said. "You want us to gain each other's skills."

"He hired me to teach you how to cheat," Rabene said. She spoke with such candor that Padmé suspected she was keeping secrets. That was all right for now, at least. Padmé had plenty of secrets of her own. "Apparently he doesn't think you are deceitful enough on your own, but I'm starting to think he's underestimated you."

Padmé smiled demurely. This was going better than she had expected. Leaving the selection up to Panaka had run the risk of him picking girls who were talented and loyal, but who weren't compatible with her particular style and goals. Somehow, both captain and Queen had gotten what they wanted: a group of handmaidens who could, hopefully, evolve into a unit to be reckoned with. Assuming, of course, their personalities were cohesive. There was a difference between ambition and commitment, and wanting to serve was not the same as being part of the whole.

"Padmé and I have already started combat training together," Tsabin said. "And I've been teaching her breathing exercises, which help control physical reactions."

Eirtama leaned forward and picked up the headpiece. Apparently she was the type who always wanted to be doing something with her hands.

"Are they all like this?" she asked, turning the piece over to examine the part that attached to Padmé's head.

"So large?" Padmé replied.

"So stiff and ungainly," she clarified. "Is this an original or a replica of a historical piece? It must be super uncomfortable."

"It is," Padmé said. "An original and uncomfortable, I mean."

"I can design one that looks exactly the same and weighs half as much," Eirtama said. "No one will know the difference except for us."

"Let me see that," Suyan said, holding out her hands. Eirtama passed the headpiece over without hesitation. "Oh, yes, we can improve this. I think it was made before Karlini silk was imported in bulk, and there's no reason we can't duplicate it in a more wearable style. This one can go in a museum or something."

"We'll look at your dresses as well." Eirtama examined the green gown Padmé wore with a critical eye. Suyan nodded. "That at least looks like it was made with modern materials, but we'll see if we can't make some modifications for comfort and functionality."

Tsabin turned expectantly to Sashah, who hadn't said anything indicating why Panaka had chosen her yet. Padmé looked at her curiously, too.

"The captain thinks we work for him," Sashah said. "He thinks of us as an extension of the Royal Security Forces. He doesn't understand what you want from us. And he has something on Rabene that he thinks he can use to control her."

That was not a surprise. Rabene shrugged.

"When he said 'artist and actress,' what he meant was that I forge classic art pieces and then convince offworlders to buy them as originals." Rabene buried a snicker. "He left out the part where I am also an accomplished musician, though. I just had to pick something at school, before they kicked me out, and I picked—"

"Crime?" Tsabin was openly laughing now. Suyan looked vaguely scandalized, but even she was smiling.

"I picked music because I'd never used it unconventionally," said Rabene deliberately.

"Of course," Tsabin said.

"Did he threaten you?" Padmé asked. She would not stand for that.

"Not in so many words," Rabene said. It didn't sound like Panaka had her worried about anything. "The school didn't press charges after they caught me, and none of the off-worlders know better. He did imply he could make it difficult for me if I said no."

"I will tell him that's inappropriate," Padmé promised.

"I don't think you should," Rabene said. "Not yet, anyway."

The six of them sat there, digesting what that meant.

"Why does he think it's so dangerous?" Suyan said. "There hasn't been an attack, direct or otherwise, on a Naboo monarch in decades. You're brilliant, but so was Sanandrassa, in her own way. So was everyone who has been queen. What does he think is coming?"

"Honestly, I think he's just paranoid," Padmé said. "He was a clerk in the legislature when he was young, and then he went into security instead of art. I know he has a passing acquaintance with Senator Palpatine, so he probably knows more about offworld politics than most other guards. I think it started as just a hunch."

"And now?" Eirtama asked.

"I'm not sure." Padmé hesitated. "We're facing a labor shortage for the harvest, which is nothing new. Debate usually goes back and forth on which solution to take, and this time the offworld buyer faction seems to be the strongest, probably because Sanandrassa supported isolationism during her reign and I've had only two weeks to start changing things. The Galactic Senate is trying to change some taxation laws, and Naboo would definitely be affected by that if anything passes. But there's no way to tell yet."

"So it's paranoia with a good direction," Rabene said.

"I don't want it to get out of control," Padmé said. "I want to be ready for anything, of course, but I don't want to be so afraid of my own shadow that I give up the parts of me that want to stay idealistic and hopeful. That's why I wanted to be queen, really. To show that Naboo can be strong in its own traditions *and* a part of the galactic community."

"We'll be your shadow," said Sashah.

Padmé looked at each of them in turn. As with Tsabin, she had already decided she was going to trust them. They had been honest with her, and they had agreed to Panaka's original terms, which included a significant confidentiality promise. They'd all given and gained to get here, to this room in the palace where they could plan the future for millions at a time, and that was common ground to start from, at the very least. When Padmé met Tsabin's eyes, the handmaiden nodded once.

"In that case, I think there are some preliminary precautions we can take," Rabene said. "I think we ought to have new names. We're all keeping secrets from our families, and everyone else on the planet, and I am *slightly* notorious, after all."

"Do you have any suggestions?" Padmé asked.

"You had to give up Padmé," Tsabin said. "What if we all chose names that sounded similar to that?"

"That would be perfect," Rabene said. "I guarantee you that most people will hear that many *ehs* in a row and literally never be able to remember how many of us there are, let alone who is who."

Eirtama clearly had objections to giving up her name but said nothing. Padmé leaned forward.

"You are allowed to disagree with me in private, you know," she said. "Especially when we're brainstorming ideas."

"I like my name," Eirtama said after a brief silence. "I was going to make it famous someday, you know? Building things or at least fixing them. I don't want to give it up."

"It has to be all of us or none, or it won't work," Rabene said. "And you can make your name famous after, if you really wanted to."

"I—" Eirtama hesitated again.

"It's very strange, to hear someone call you by a new

name," Padmé said. "It took me a while to get used to. I didn't have a choice, so I won't make yours for you."

"The point is to be invisible," Sashah said. "If you want to be famous, this isn't the job for you."

Eirtama straightened up at the critique, like she had been issued a direct challenge.

"I can do both," she insisted. She slumped in acceptance, not quite defeat. "But you're right about waiting. I won't be the youngest to do anything, I guess, but I can still be the best."

It was clear Eirtama wasn't thrilled, but the first obstacle had been crossed.

"When you're in makeup, we should always call you Your Highness," Suyan suggested, clearing her throat to change the subject. Sashah looked at her and then quickly averted her eyes. "That will help establish boundaries and let us know when we're allowed to argue about things. Even if we're alone."

"We'll all wear the makeup at some point, I think," Tsabin said. "Even if it's only for practice."

"Whoever wears the face gets the title," Eirtama said. She seemed determined to help make decisions, if only to make sure they were the ones she agreed with. It was better than nothing. "And we'll practice not being shocked if some palace page addresses us in company."

"Speaking of pages," Sashah said. "I think I should be

one. You'll need someone who can run errands and not be suspicious because people see her all the time. I'm the smallest and the least likely to be the Queen. I'm the best choice."

Padmé turned over all the suggestions in her head. They were coming together better than she could have hoped, and they were only getting started.

"I think Padmé should be a page, too," Rabene said.

"How would that work?" Tsabin asked.

"If there's magically another girl around the Queen, someone might notice," Rabene said. "People should get used to seeing her. No one pays attention to pages."

"I think that's a direct contradiction," Tsabin said. "But I also think you're right."

Panaka would never allow it. The idea of Padmé wandering around Theed as herself would push the captain too far. She was sure of it. But perhaps he would understand why that role would be a good one for her to play inside the palace walls. He was a reasonable person, and Rabene's logic was sound.

"We'll ease him into it," Sashah said, discerning the problem. "And I'll be the primary page, anyway, which will help."

They were all grinning openly now, delighted by the scheme they were weaving, the secrets they would hold close between them.

"Rabé," Rabene said. "Your wardrobe mistress, I think."

That would give her access to the most personal items

that protected the Queen—her clothes, jewelry, and other accessories—and provide a reason for her to always be on hand. It was perfect for an intelligence officer.

"Yané," said Suyan. "I'll be in charge of liaising with the palace staff and droids."

She would have her finger on the pulse of everything that went on inside the walls. No one would suspect anything abnormal if she was to appear suddenly in the kitchens or gardens to talk to someone about the Queen's needs.

"Eirtaé," Eirtama said. "Communications."

Everyone would be used to seeing her with a variety of tech in her hands. They wouldn't think about what she was doing with it.

"Saché. The lowly page."

No one would think much about seeing her at all.

Each girl had chosen something that would make them seem completely harmless, yet would also allow them to have additional functions without causing anyone to look twice. Their skills could be brought into play without anyone being the wiser.

Padmé smiled and looked at Tsabin. Her first handmaiden. In the two weeks since the election, they had spent nearly every moment together, though most people hadn't been entirely aware of Tsabin's presence. She had offered opinions on a variety of matters, and Padmé was already coming to rely on Tsabin's good sense to temper her own idealism.

They were friends, or they were on their way to friendship. And they were learning to navigate the power imbalance between them. It wasn't perfect—Saché seemed to be avoiding Yané deliberately—but it was a start.

"I will be everyone's assistant," Tsabin said. "That way people will get used to my stepping into random roles, and also not question my absence if I'm not visible."

"And?" Padmé asked. Tsabin would always have to follow the choices of others. The least they could do was give her this.

Tsabin smiled.

"Sabé."

CHAPTER 7

"I don't like it," Panaka said.

"It's your own fault, dear," Mariek told him. She was always blunt, and usually he really liked that about her, but it was a less attractive quality when she was pointing out his own shortcomings. "You can't put that many teenage girls together and not expect them to scheme. Or kill each other. Frankly, you're lucky they appear to be doing the former."

Panaka thought of about nine responses to that, eight of which would probably end in divorce. He gave up and tried another tack.

"Do you have any suggestions on how to deal with them?" he asked. "Since you appear to be an expert."

"Because I was one, you mean?" she said wickedly.

"I—"

"I'm kidding, love," she said. "You've given the Queen an excellent toolbox. What she does with it is up to her, unfortunately for your poor nerves, but the box is still yours. Just don't make it a cage, or they'll really turn on you."

"I'm not caging them!" he said.

"Call it whatever you want," Mariek said. "You're

controlling them, and they won't like that any more than you like that they're controlling you. Just do your job and trust them."

"I wish you'd taken the promotion to the personal guard," Panaka groused.

"That would have been a terrible idea," Mariek said. "Since I mostly agree with them in this scenario."

She kissed him, laughing, and Panaka was left with the sinking feeling that he'd lost more than one fight that morning.

⟩♡♡⟨

The first problem was that Saché refused to share a room with Yané.

She gave no reason and dug in her heels with a stubbornness no one had anticipated. Rabé and Eirtaé had concocted some sort of randomizer for the schedule, the idea being that no one handmaiden was ever in the same place two days in a row, and Saché's fit was preventing them from implementing it. Padmé was reluctant to take sides, mostly because Yané was inexplicably in agreement with Saché. It seemed intensely personal in a way Padmé didn't entirely understand, and it was foolish, but she was determined to give her handmaidens what privacy she could, and if this was all Saché ever required, it wasn't that much.

"Fine," Rabé declared at last. "We'll just add it to the

randomizer program. You'll never have to sleep in the same room. I'm assuming you're all right being seen in public together?"

Saché conceded gracefully, and the next three days saw Rabé's favorite sweets sent up with their evening tea, which everyone considered an adequate apology.

Panaka wasn't entirely pleased that he never knew how many hooded figures would be escorting the Queen on any given day. That had been Rabé's idea, too. If the Queen was always accompanied by a different number of handmaidens, it would be more difficult to tell who was absent at any given time.

"There are five of them to protect you," Panaka said. His voice was carefully controlled, as was the Queen's. They were both trying to speak in such a way that respect was as clear as disagreement, but they hadn't had quite enough practice yet.

"This is how they will protect me," Amidala countered.

In the end, Padmé agreed to two more guards being added to each shift. It was the rare compromise where everyone got what they wanted in the first place, and the cost was deemed acceptable by all parties.

By the end of the second week, Yané declared it was time to give Sabé the chance to leave the suite in the Queen's face. She'd memorized the staff rotation and made a note of the schedule on which the droids cleaned the floors and windows. She knew exactly what timing such an expedition should have.

Furthermore, she and Eirtaé had finished three new head-pieces, in addition to their other duties, and a dress that had all the appearance of a traditional Naboo gown at one-third the weight. The new gown had much easier fasteners, making it simpler to get in and out of, which Rabé had insisted on after they showed her the original designs.

They picked a morning when Amidala had no public appearances. Saché left the suite and returned three times on various errands, and then Padmé, dressed identically, left to ostensibly get a book from the Queen's library, which was located at the end of the hallway. All Sabé had to do was make it down the hall without being recognized for it to be a successful test.

"This actually weighs less than the old ones?" Sabé asked as Yané fitted the shoulder pieces and tabard over the enormous blue gown.

"Don't be petty," Rabé said. "You know how hard they worked on this."

Sabé wore a set of light blue robes beneath the dress, the same set Saché and Padmé had worn when they were seen leaving the room. The handmaidens usually wore robes in the same style, set to complement whatever the Queen was wearing. Hoods were quickly coming into fashion, spreading from the court to Theed to the general populace, and at any given time, there were several handmaiden-looking women in any part of the palace.

Over the robes, Sabé wore a dark blue dress made of Karlini silk and cut to match an archaic Naboo style. Her tabard was black, and held down by an elaborately jeweled belt. The massive shoulder pieces, which would do most of the work in terms of supporting the headpiece, were also black. Eirtaé was not entirely happy with the design, but Yané had convinced her that it would be easier to test a physical model rather than just keep sketching it over and over again. The headpiece itself was a deceptively simple hairstyle wreathed in white and blue beads that rattled whenever Sabé moved her head. A wide triangular piece rested against the back of her shoulders and the back of her head, completing the look. It didn't do much for her peripheral vision, but her posture was impeccable.

Yané finished the last few brushstrokes of makeup.

"That should do it," she declared. "What do you think?"

Rabé and Eirtaé both examined her closely and offered no comment.

"The shoulders are a good idea," Saché said. "No one will pay too much attention to her face, even if they try. Their eyes will always be drawn off."

"Thank you," Yané said. She took off the apron she'd used to keep the face powder off her robes and pulled the hood up over her head. She and Eirtaé would be the ones to accompany Sabé on the test, because the other half of it was seeing if they could switch Padmé back into the Queen's face while they were in the library.

"Let's go," Sabé said.

"Of course, Your Highness," Rabé said, not blinking as she stared into Sabé's painted face.

It was going to take more than that to rattle the second-best girl. Sabé nodded slowly, and turned to the door.

The guards in the hallway straightened when Amidala walked past them, and gave no indication that they spotted anything unusual. Two of them fell in behind Yané and Eirtaé. It was about fifty meters down the hall to the library, and the distance suddenly seemed ridiculously far to Sabé. The dress was heavy. She hadn't practiced enough in the shoes. She couldn't turn her head because of the headpiece. She filled her lungs, no part of her moving to reveal the steadying breath, and started walking.

They got within ten meters of the door before Captain Panaka appeared in the hallway. He was early. Behind Sabé, Yané inhaled sharply and Eirtaé subtly grimaced.

"Your Highness," Panaka said amicably. "I didn't think you had any appointments today."

"I am going to the library," Sabé said, hoping to keep the conversation as brief as possible.

Panaka nodded and stepped aside to let them pass. He was almost past Sabé's eyeline when she saw his brow furrow. She took the last few paces to the library as quickly as she could, letting Eirtaé pass her to get the door open. This gave Eirtaé a clear view of Panaka's face as Amidala went into the room before she shut the guards out.

Sabé wanted to lean back against the door and grumble, but the dress wouldn't let her. She settled for cursing under her breath instead.

"It could have gone worse," Yané said encouragingly.

"What happened?" Padmé asked. The "page" was standing on top of the library ladder, a book in her hand so that if anyone else came in, she could pretend to have just located it.

"Panaka," Sabé said shortly. She held out her arms so that Eirtaé could get to work.

Padmé came down the ladder and stood in front of her so that Yané could start the prep, too.

"He caught you?" she asked.

"He saw us," Sabé said. "And I am sure he knows it was me."

"He was puzzling it through, in any case," Eirtaé said. "When I saw his face, he was still thinking."

"Which was all you needed," Padmé said. "That's not bad for a first try."

Sabé didn't reply, hypothetically because Eirtaé was wiping the makeup off her face, but truly because, just once, she had wanted to be the best at something because of a natural gift.

"He only started to suspect when you spoke," Yané said.

"I can't double for the Queen if I can't speak," Sabé said.

Her head was free of the headpiece, so she twisted her hair up into the simple coil the handmaidens were wearing in readiness for the hood.

"We've talked about the Queen's face," Padmé said. "We do that with makeup and practice mirroring each other's expressions. We'll just . . . have to come up with the Queen's voice."

It wasn't a terrible idea.

"You already speak differently when you talk to government officials," Sabé said. "It shouldn't be too hard to adjust the inflection for both of us."

"All of us, I'll say, because Rabé isn't here," Padmé said. She was smiling. Sabé had thought she might be disappointed, but the truth was that Padmé loved a plan, and now they had one. "And we'll have to work to incorporate Rabé's accent as well."

"I'll add it to the list," Eirtaé said.

Working quickly, the handmaidens transferred the dress from one queen to the other, and Yané produced a small, portable version of the royal makeup case from one of her pockets. She did Padmé's face while Eirtaé attached the headpiece and Sabé tucked herself into her hood. It took several minutes to make the changeover. If it was a more complicated dress, like any of the ones Amidala wore for court, it wouldn't have been so quick, but Rabé insisted they work their way up to that challenge.

Sabé picked up the book Padmé had retrieved, and fell

into place at the back of the procession. Eirtaé opened the door again, and the four of them progressed into the hallway as though it were any other sort of day.

This time, the fifty meters seemed friendlier. All Sabé had to do was keep her head down, and pass for the page everyone had seen enter the library half an hour ago. The guards fell into step behind her, and they all walked back to the suite as though everything was perfectly normal. When they reached the door, Panaka threw it open for them.

"Did you find the book you wanted, Your Highness?" he asked blandly.

They hadn't told him about the plan to make Padmé a separate identity as a page. Yané had said it was easier to ask forgiveness than permission, so they had just gone ahead and done it. Perhaps they should have left the "page" in the library to better sell the bit. Eirtaé could add that to the list.

"Yes, thank you, Captain," Padmé said. Her voice was pitched low, much closer to Sabé's than usual. "I did."

⚊⚌⚌⚊

Governor Bibble was not surprised by the result of the vote, but Padmé could tell he was a bit disappointed, though neither she nor her handmaidens gave any indication.

"Of course we all understand the agricultural reasons for allowing half the fields on Naboo to rot," he said after they finished summarizing the report. "There is always a risk of overfarming, and any chance to help the nitrogen cycle along naturally is appreciated—but I had hoped that your influence would be enough to unlock the planet, such as it were."

"I agree, Governor," Amidala said. The new voice didn't come naturally to her quite yet, so they were trying it out on a known ally to start with. So far, Bibble hadn't reacted at all. "The economy could certainly support buying grain right now, but there is a difference between simply purchasing things from offworlders and actually welcoming them, as encouraging emigration from offworld would have done."

Sanandrassa had been a good ruler, but she had shuttered Naboo in keeping with her beliefs about planetary isolationism, and both Queen and governor had been looking forward to opening it up again. Neither of them needed to say it out loud.

"Ah, well," Bibble said quietly as Amidala rose to take her leave. "There's always next season."

"We appreciate your dedication, Governor," Amidala said. Her voice cracked slightly at the end of the sentence.

"Are you feeling well, Your Highness?" Bibble asked. "You have adjusted to being queen exceptionally well, but there are always strange side effects to new jobs."

"I am quite fine, thank you," Amidala said. She let a bit of warmth back into the queen's tone. A movement in the corner of her eye caught her attention, and she knew Yané had balled up her hands in her sleeves, which she often did when she was trying not to laugh.

"I'll let you know the developments as I receive them," Bibble said, bowing to her.

Once the door was closed between them, Padmé heard the unmistakable sound of a snicker from inside Rabé's hood.

CHAPTER 8

The situation between Saché and Yané didn't change, nor did it become any clearer what the situation actually was. They were friendly enough to each other, but Saché would not be left alone with the older girl. She refused to explain why, and Yané did not seem to take offense. Gentle teasing only made Saché uncomfortable and caused Yané to shut down, so eventually the others just gave up and accepted it as a personality quirk. Like Eirtaé's tinkering with small electronics or Rabé's tendency to whistle when she was thinking, they ignored the issues completely. Which is to say: the annoyances built up until they exploded in a semispectacular fashion.

"I *thought* you would appreciate the chance to write a more complicated program," Yané snapped. Eirtaé was grumbling about having to move out of the room when Saché caught the cold Yané had picked up the week previously. The med-droid had recommended the two of them share a room until their symptoms passed. Saché had refused point-blank.

"My life is complicated enough, thank you," Eirtaé said. "I could be apprenticing in the eastern quadrants, helping to build bridges, but instead I'm here with the pair of *you*, and you can't even be *sick* together."

For a moment, it looked like Padmé was going to pull rank, something she had never done in the suite. But then Saché sighed.

"I'm sorry," she said. "I'll move in with Yané."

"I have already *packed*!" Eirtaé was well into high dudgeon now. Since they so rarely got to vent their emotions, it was probably overdue.

"Packed what, exactly?" Sabé asked. "We share a closet."

Eirtaé looked ready to bite someone's head off, and Padmé reluctantly stepped in.

"Thank you, Saché, for seeing the other side of this," she said. It came out in the lower tone they'd been working on for Amidala. "I know it's not easy to do something that makes you uncomfortable."

Saché slunk off to the room where Yané had been staying since she started showing symptoms.

"Eirtaé, I'm sorry for the disruption," Padmé said.

"Don't you take the blame for this," Eirtaé said. "I'm not supposed to be angry with you."

"You can be angry in here," Padmé said. "Festering serves no one."

"Thank you," Eirtaé said. She did not apologize or accept Padmé's apology, but that was the price of common living.

"Do you really want to build bridges?" Padmé asked. They

had loosely agreed that the handmaidens would stay at least one term, but no one had made any binding promises.

"Not really," Eirtaé said. She grinned. "Bridges are easy."

"Anyone else?" asked Padmé. "Since we're all here."

There were a few moments of silence, and then Sabé cleared her throat.

"I don't want to make it look like we're piling on Saché," she said carefully. "But she's not very good at the voice."

The Queen's voice had been a rising point of contention all week. Since Padmé had tuned it to Sabé without thinking it through, the other three were forced to match Sabé's tones despite their higher voices. It was difficult for all of them, particularly Rabé. She'd already developed an accent for school to mask the fact that she'd come from the Western Provinces, and the Queen's voice required an entirely new way of speaking. Still, she was making progress, and it was Saché who was struggling the most. There was only so much her vocal cords could do.

She slouched back into the room, wearing a mask over her mouth and nose.

"I know," she said miserably. "I just can't, I think, and we'll all have to accept it. There's no point in changing the whole plan because one of us can't do it. I'll just never be the Queen."

Rabé considered it. Ideally, every one of them should be working to become mirrors of each other, but it was proving harder in practice than it was in theory. There was no hiding Saché's small stature, even with the cleverest of shoes, and Eirtaé's blond hair made things challenging as well.

"Fine," she said, and turned to Eirtaé. "Will that affect your algorithm?"

"Oh, to hell with the algorithm," Sabé said. "I'm sick of planning every move and pretending to be each other so that we can fool the guards now and everyone else in an emergency that might never happen."

"It's not that simple, Sabé," Yané said. She also had a mask over the lower part of her face. It didn't hide the concern in her eyes. Of all of them, she was the one with the most emotional attachment to the group, it seemed. She hated it when they squabbled, and she did her best to mediate every situation she could. The fact that she was too sick to do that right now wasn't her fault, but the others knew she still saw it as a personal failure. "Captain Panaka brought us here to be ready, and the Queen let us choose how we're going to do it. We knew what we were signing on for when we took the job."

"So we change the job," Padmé said. "We haven't been at this long enough to perfect it. What should we do instead?"

They considered it for a while. Rabé turned scenarios over in her head, but they were all too similar to what they were already trying. Sabé had no suggestion at all, just a restlessness that wouldn't leave her alone.

"We've been trying to be like each other physically." Saché

said it in the voice she used when she was thinking out loud. Since no one else had any ideas, they let her run with it. "We've practiced walking and talking and dressing and standing and thinking. What if we tried . . . something more practical?"

"How much more practical than walking can you get?" Eirtaé asked. The confrontation had drained out of her tone.

"In the evenings, before bed," Saché said. "We sit around and talk or read. What if it was someone's task to read out loud, and the rest of us learned each other's hobbies? We pick up extra skills, it gives us something to do, and it might let us understand the way each of us thinks."

"I can show you how to pick locks," Rabé said.

"That's not really a hobby," Yané said.

"None of the things I do for fun are hobbies," Rabé said. "At least lock picking might come in handy someday."

"That's a start," Saché said. "Padmé?"

Padmé considered it. Saché's point was a good one. They were learning each other's skin, but not each other's heart. The closeness she'd found with Sabé in those first two weeks when it had just been the two of them, talking in the dark, had yet to be replicated with the others. This might be a good way of closing those gaps, forming those bonds.

"All right," she said, and smiled. "Lock picking first."

91

From then on, it got a little easier. Their days were still full of conforming to a single identity that wasn't any of them, exactly, but their evenings were their own. If Captain Panaka wondered why the Queen had requisitioned several complicated lockplates and then a wide selection of embroidery threads immediately afterward, he didn't ask. The girls assumed he didn't want to know, and were more or less correct.

Amidala left for a tour of the agricultural provinces a few days after they settled into their new pattern. All of the handmaidens went with her, dressed in flame-colored robes and placed throughout the column so that no one knew exactly who was where at any given moment. The page named Padmé was also included in the travel log, with some protest from Panaka. He didn't mind the "page" accompanying the party, but he was reluctant to make her existence public record. They compromised again: Padmé was officially registered, but she was rarely seen by anyone, since her supposed task as the Queen's primary archivist for the trip kept her out of the way.

The Queen traveled with considerable accompaniment. Governor Bibble went with her, along with Graf Zapalo, the agricultural advisor; Horace Vancil, the economic advisor; and all of their staff. Additional security forces were added. Panaka had limited the number of transports to seven, which finally capped the number of people who could be brought along. The eighth vehicle in their retinue contained the Queen's wardrobe.

The Queen rode in an open speeder with the governor beside her. It was her first appearance in public outside the capital, and her citizens were eager to see her. Every morning, Rabé painted her face and Eirtaé strapped her into whatever royal regalia Yané declared was particularly important to the region they were passing through. Sabé stood in for her only once, the morning Padmé's period started and she spent the first few hours of the day in bed waiting for the painkillers to kick in. Aside from that, they decided that it was important for the people of Naboo to see the real Queen, since so many of them had voted for her.

"How are you not on the suppressant shots?" Rabé asked once Padmé was on her feet and they had an opportunity to switch her back in.

"It's not usually this bad," Padmé admitted. It was deeply embarrassing to be caught off guard by one's own body, even if Sabé had done a perfect job of filling in for her.

"You are under more stress than usual," Yané said. "I'll add it to your medical profile, and the droids will take care of it when we get back."

By the fifth day, they had passed more fields of rotting grain than Padmé ever wanted to see. They had explained it to her, and she had some understanding of it in the first place, even if the exact chemical makeup of the soil had been something she hadn't known before. It was sound agricultural practice. Soon the farmers would plough the rotted stalks back into the ground, and the fields would be replenished. The minister of finance was along on the trip to reassure everyone that they would be properly compensated, and between the promise of currency and the presence of the Queen, there was a certain festival atmosphere to the whole thing.

It smelled, though. And the smell was inescapable. It permeated everything and made her think of rot and ruin and waste. None of those were things that she was comfortable with, but it was important that Amidala be seen to approve of the decision the government had made.

"Where are we planning to purchase grain from?" Amidala asked Zapalo one afternoon while they rode in the open speeder. There were only eight seats, and Padmé's dress took a whole row, so it was just her, the governor, the advisors, Panaka, Bibble's chief aide, and Saché.

"We're still considering that, Your Highness," he said. "Several worlds have been approached and we expect all of them to make a bid. Then we'll negotiate for the best deal."

"Did we approach Karlinus or Jafan?" Amidala named the two planets in the Chommell sector most renowned for agricultural output.

"No, Your Highness." Zapalo seemed surprised. "We didn't. Karlinus, as you know, has focused primarily on tea and silk these past few years. I am not sure if they have a surplus big enough to support us. And Jafan definitely does not."

"It doesn't have to support us entirely," Amidala said. The

new voice made people uncomfortable because it made her even harder to read. It was, she admitted, a large part of the appeal. "If we can support their economies, even if it's only a bit, I think it's a matter worth exploring."

The advisors exchanged looks and then turned to Bibble. His aide was already tapping on his recorder.

"There's no reason we can't look into it, Your Highness," Bibble said. "And I also think reaching out to our neighbors first is a good approach. We can't rely on them entirely, but we can see if there's a chance for a mutually beneficial deal."

"Very well," Vancil said. "I'll have my people begin the process of coordinating with the agriculture ministry as soon as we get back to Theed."

"Thank you." The Queen was always gracious, and let the conversation turn to subjects her advisors found less intimidating.

⟆⩗⩗⟆

Saché, whose page persona was so unexceptional that most of the government officials had already stopped paying attention to her unless they needed something, was perched on the jump seat at the front of the car and faced backward. She had the clearest view of everyone's faces. Bibble was pleased. Panaka was carefully neutral. Neither of the advisors was thrilled, but they weren't openly opposed. It was Padmé's face that was the most interesting, though. While the others clearly considered the matter closed for now, Padmé was still turning it over. She turned her face upward, like she was enjoying the sun, but Saché knew better. She was thinking of the other planets in the sector. And she wasn't going to stop until she had what she wanted.

Padmé met her gaze when she looked down, and Saché nodded, barely moving her head. Whatever it was, the handmaidens would help her get it.

CHAPTER 9

The apprentice sat in the dark, waiting for his master's call. He'd lingered in the shadows for years now, ever since he had been chosen, and it was starting to grate on his nerves. He knew that was intentional. It made him angry to wait, to be pushed to the side while his master manipulated the galaxy without him. It made him feel unwanted, and worse: unneeded. And, of course, that made him angry, too.

Maul had mastered anger a long time ago. He'd wrestled with it in the deep caves of Dathomir as a child, and he'd wrestled so loudly that it had drawn his master's attention. Most would have let the anger burn them up. Most would have flared out in glorious rage, taking untold numbers with them into the blackness of the void, but not Maul. Maul was made for better things, and his anger was his fuel.

He was still working on hatred.

There were just so many things to hate. He hated the way the fog on Dathomir had clouded his vision and made the witches stronger. He hated the way he had been cast aside as a male-child until some offworlder saw his use. He hated that same offworlder for training him so astutely, through such pain and suffering, and then not letting him loose to wreak the same upon the galaxy. Most of all, he hated the Jedi.

They hadn't come for him. He didn't know if they had sensed him and found him unworthy, or if, in his untrained state, he hadn't been worth their time, but it didn't matter. They had ignored him, passed him over for some unknown reason, and even though he had been better served by their neglect—he was more powerful with his anger than he could have been without it—he counted the days until he could make them pay.

The pieces of his lightsaber hovered in the air in front of him, separated from the wholeness while he tinkered with the alignment for the hundredth time. The lightsaber was death. This, too, was something he had been forced to grapple for. Every part of it was stolen, and every part of it was irrevocably *his*, paid for in blood and pain, only some of which had been his own. He focused, calling on the well of darkness inside him, the parts that had scared the younger witches and now delighted his master so much. With the ease of much practice, he pulled the saber together, the parts aligning as easily as everything else in his life had not. When it was completed, he stretched out a hand, pressed the button, and lost himself in the hum.

If asked, Maul would say he feared nothing.

He was wrong.

⟩♥♥♥⟨

Chancellor Valorum did not enjoy meetings with the Trade Federation. He was not allowed to admit it in public, but he harbored a vague distaste for senators who represented corporations, not planets. It was an outdated viewpoint, which was just one of the reasons he had to keep his dislike a secret. Most of the galaxy believed that a person's employer had just as much right to a place in the government as a person did. But that didn't mean he had to like it. Only that he must, in his current position, pretend to.

The tax situation was starting to get ridiculous. Any other bill that had failed in the Senate so many times would have been shoved under a rug by now, but for some reason, variations on this one kept coming back. It was not unlike being haunted, except instead of a ghost that might be exorcised, it was bureaucrats that just would *not* stop talking about it.

"You cannot expect the Mid Rim planets to accept that!" Senator Palpatine argued, barely bothering to moderate his tone for the chancellor's office. "They don't have coffers that deep."

This was the fourth committee meeting Valorum had hosted in the hope of avoiding a general brawl in the Senate chambers. The blue-shrouded senatorial guards inspired some sense of decorum from the delegates, and the wide windows kept the atmosphere light and airy. So far, at least, it had all been for naught: nothing had been agreed upon.

"The Trade Federation is happy to offer aid to any planet that requires it," Lott Dodd fired back. "We have been over that several times, Senator."

Senator Yarua, the Wookiee delegate, said something too quickly for Valorum to understand. The speaker's emotions were clear enough, but Valorum looked down to the screen to get the translation.

"No, Senator," Palpatine said. "I don't think the terms of that aid would be very attractive either."

A chime sounded from the comm system, indicating that the allotted time for the meeting was over. Everyone had somewhere else to be. Valorum did his best not to look too put out. At this stage, a floor fight was starting to look inevitable.

"Walk with me, Senator," he said to Palpatine as the others filed out. The Neimoidians looked affronted, but Valorum was trusted enough to be beyond such petty accusations of favoritism. Still, he sent Mas Amedda with the trade delegation in the hope that the presence of the vice chair would make them feel better.

"I apologize, Chancellor," Palpatine said as the two men made their way down the corridor toward the senator's office. "I didn't mean to be so aggressive in there."

"It's your own planet," Valorum said with some sympathy. "No one can blame you for feeling a bit emotional about it."

"Thank you," Palpatine said.

"Do you think we would benefit at all from having an independent moderator step in?" Valorum asked.

"A Jedi, you mean?" Palpatine said, appearing surprised. "I hadn't thought of that. I don't think we're that far gone, sir, and I'd hate to impinge upon senatorial privilege until we needed to."

"You're probably right," Valorum said. The Jedi were a good solution, but a very extreme one. It wouldn't do to call them in over a trade dispute before all the arguments were presented. That was the sort of thing that happened *outside* of Coruscant.

They reached Palpatine's office, and the senator took his leave. Valorum continued back to his chambers. It was good to have sensible allies.

𝄞𝄡𝄡𝄢

Shmi Skywalker watched as her son's podracer caught fire and crashed into a dune. She wanted to scream, to rage that Watto made him do it when it wasn't safe. No other humans had ever competed in a podrace, and Anakin's dubious record was in jeopardy every time he waited at the start line. But she could do nothing. She couldn't protest or argue, couldn't barter or trade. She had nothing of her own to give.

Except Anakin himself, of course, which Watto already knew and took advantage of at every turn.

The med-droids reached the podracer right after the fire suppressors kicked in, and Shmi could see them pulling apart the tangled metal in search of a survivor. At least he hadn't been thrown this time. He'd crashed on a rocky part of the raceway, not that sand was much softer when you hit it at speed. Even aflame, the podracer was moderately safer than a body slam into the ground.

Watto hovered over, the flap of his wings giving him away long before he reached her, even though she didn't turn around.

"The boy's fine," he said. "Like always."

"Someday it won't be always, Watto," Shmi said.

"Maybe someday he'll stop ruining my podracer, too," Watto said, laughing. He flew off to collect his winnings—he never bet on his own, obviously—and Shmi resumed waiting for the med-droids to finish.

Shmi went to the racing pit where they would bring him. She was a familiar face down there. Droids weren't exactly known for their sympathetic glances, but she felt like they were all giving them to her as she walked to the medical area. She arrived just before Anakin did.

He was on a stretcher. It dwarfed his small form, and they quickly transferred him to a cot. He didn't appear to be bleeding too badly, but Shmi couldn't tell if he'd injured anything internally.

"It's okay, Mom," he said when he saw her. He was still full of adrenaline, beyond pain and riding the high of the race. He loved it so much, and he had so few things to love. This was the real reason she could never deny him.

"Ani," she said. She ruffled his hair.

"They're just going to put me out while the bacta knits my femurs," he chirruped.

Shmi lifted the cover and saw that both his legs were twisted. That, at least, Watto would happily pay to fix.

"Don't worry, Mom," Anakin said. "I'm always going to be with you."

He reached for her hand, and she took it. It was ridiculous that she accepted this as comfort in this situation—lately Anakin was embarrassed when she mothered him in public—but she didn't know what else to do. If she started screaming, she would never stop.

"You'll have to step back now, ma'am," the droid said.

The medical droids were rustic, but efficient. Before long, Anakin was unconscious and they were working on his legs. Shmi had to look away when the bones started moving. There was only so much her heart could take.

"Someday it won't be always," she said. And it was a promise to them both.

Yoda sat in a small garden in the Jedi Temple where he was usually left alone. Today, however, his meditations were interrupted by Mace Windu, who had come all the way out to talk to him even though they had just been in the Council chamber a few hours before.

"Questions not fit for the others, you have?" Yoda asked as Windu took a seat on the grass beside him. "Embarrassing, are they?"

"No, Master Yoda," Windu said. He had never responded well to Yoda's particular brand of humor, even as a youngling. It was one of the reasons Yoda kept it up.

Yoda let him sit on it for a while longer, until finally the younger Jedi cracked.

"You sense something," Windu said. "Something you haven't told anyone else about."

"So clever you are, Master Windu," Yoda said. "And so close to the truth. But think you not in the right direction, I say."

"What other direction is there, Master?" Windu asked. "Either you sense something or you sense nothing."

Yoda took another moment to not reply. If he waited long enough, they almost always figured it out on their own. It was his favorite method of teaching.

"You sense nothing," Windu said after a while. "Master, there is always *some*thing."

"Open your mind, Master Windu," Yoda said. "If sensed nothing is, something must it be."

Windu leaned forward, resting elbows on knees and chin in hands. He managed to make it look graceful, which was not always easy for human males.

"No," he said finally. "Nothing can never be something. They are opposites."

"So sure you are," Yoda said. "Reassuring, it is. Never so sure of myself am I."

"You think differently?" Windu said. It was starting to feel like a debate with Qui-Gon, and neither of them really enjoyed those.

"I think I sense nothing," Yoda said. "Presume anything after that, I do not."

Yoda waited while Windu thought through his next question. There was no point in asking if Yoda was afraid, because he would only turn the question back, and Windu didn't enjoy that sort of exposure. All he could do was follow his lessons, the ones he had received as a boy and given as a Knight and Master in the Temple. He must let it go. The Force would tell him when it was time, and he must not allow himself to be distracted by Yoda's behaviors.

"I trust your judgment, Master Yoda," he said at last. "I know if there is an answer, you will find it."

Yoda didn't respond. Instead, he closed his eyes and reached for the calm of the living Force flowing through him. After a few minutes, he felt Windu get up and leave him alone with his thoughts, which was his favorite place to be.

The light surrounded him, the dark a comfortable distance from the limits of his perception. And yet there was something; rather, there was nothing. And it eluded him completely.

CHAPTER 10

The sunlight through the windows of the throne room gave the marble an opalescent sheen. The glass had been treated to throw rainbows against the ceiling when the light caught it at certain angles, and the wall hangings were muted colors to allow anyone in the room to fully appreciate them. Occasionally, the decorations in the room served as a distraction from what was going on within it, but today no one was looking anywhere other than at the Queen.

Amidala was clad in purple. Her underdress was completely covered by the stiff velvet of her outermost layer, except at her collar, where soft lavender curled around her neck. For the rest, she might have been a statue. The dress was embroidered so heavily that it weighed itself down, instead of using tricks around the hem to make sure everything stayed in place. A deep green sash completed the look. The style was a little severe, which was reflected in Amidala's stoic expression, and the Queen was covered from wrists to ankles. Her headpiece was unusually simple, consisting of a wig that had been styled with coiled braids in a crown, each highlighted by purple and green gems. A silver comb had been tucked into the back of the braid crown, and a purple veil hung down behind her head.

It had taken Rabé and Eirtaé nearly an hour to secure all the pins that held it in place. Padmé was almost afraid to move her head.

Queen Amidala had requested the presence of the governor and several advisors today. None of them had turned her down, naturally, even though she had given no reason for her summons.

"Governor, representatives," Queen Amidala said. There was no mistaking the voice now. It was pitched low and grated a bit, but it definitely attracted attention. "We thank you for attending us today."

"Of course, Your Highness," Bibble said.

"We wished to inform you that we will be hosting a summit at the Royal Palace in two weeks' time," Amidala continued. Since this was news to everyone, they all appeared a bit startled.

"A summit for whom?" the minister of internal affairs asked. After a moment, she added, "Your Highness."

Amidala nodded to show there were no hard feelings.

"For our counterparts on other planets in the Chommell sector," she said.

There was a long silence at that.

"Your Highness," Bibble said reluctantly. He looked

desperately uncomfortable. "You're the only queen in the Chommell sector."

"You misunderstand us, perhaps, Governor," Amidala said graciously. "Allow a clarification: we will invite the politicians from those planets who serve as heads of state, regardless of the titles they hold."

"Your Highness," said Graf Zapalo, "why?"

"It has come to our attention that our trade overtures were not well received," Amidala said. This was a slight understatement. Karlinus had immediately responded that they had no surplus, and Jafan had failed to respond at all. "We wanted to invite our counterparts here so that we might discuss matters in person and discover where the problem lies."

They couldn't actually stop her. They could make her life difficult, which was why she was telling them at all, but they couldn't prevent the summit from happening. All they could do was voice their displeasure and make her explain herself in very small words.

"Your Highness," Bibble said, "surely the matter of a bit of grain is not so important that we have to take such drastic measures. It could be seen as confrontational."

She had expected Bibble to be her staunchest ally in this matter. It was well known that he was as interested in reopening interplanetary relations as she was. In a flash, she knew: he was letting her win them over. Once he stopped protesting, they wouldn't have any defense left.

"It isn't just the grain, Governor," Amidala said. "I want to talk about all trade and relations between the planets in our system."

"It's a lofty goal," Bibble said, conceding the point. "And a worthwhile one, I think."

"Captain Panaka." Amidala turned slightly to address him. "Do you have anything to say?"

There was no reason at all to ask her head of security to weigh in at this point. Panaka didn't hold a legislative position, and he had no say in any decision the Queen came to in terms of policy. Rabé had suggested they ask him in public, however, and Sabé had agreed. He wouldn't be able to argue too much if there were witnesses.

"There would be a lot to organize, Your Highness," he said slowly. He knew what they were up to, and they could discuss the practical details later, with fewer witnesses. "In addition to any palace security, we would have to have plans in place for any excursions you took the visitors on."

"We would take your suggestions into account for anything outside the palace." It was her peace offering. "You know best the problems we might face."

She waited to see what Panaka would do. He took a moment, and then proved Rabé correct.

"While I don't think the security of the Queen has anything to do with the summit directly," he said, "any relations in the sector would involve planetary security, and that affects both the Queen and the rest of you. It's not an openly defensive move, but it doesn't make us look vulnerable either."

"Thank you, Captain," Amidala said. She turned back to the advisors.

They looked uncomfortable, but they were out of arguments. She had won, so she could afford to be gracious. She'd do her best to make the summit bother them as little as possible.

"Your Highness," Zapalo said. "We will await further direction on how we may assist you in this matter."

"Thank you," Amidala said.

Bibble reminded them that they had a legislative vote that afternoon, and they took their leave as a group. None of them was grumbling too noticeably, at least. Amidala waited for the room to clear before she turned back to Panaka.

"Captain," she said.

"I don't love it," he said. "But I can see why you want to do it."

"Thank you for your support," Amidala said. "I'm sorry we surprised you along with them."

She would've sworn she heard one of the other guards muffle a laugh.

"I do welcome your suggestions, Captain," she said.

"I'll come up with more than a few, I'm sure," Panaka said.

Padmé didn't doubt it for a second.

Panaka's list was not as extensive as she had feared. Most of it was common sense. The blast doors that protected the throne room, for example. They were all tested, and when one of them was found to be faulty, the mechanism was replaced. A survey of the palace and grounds was conducted, looking for weak spots in Panaka's grid, and right behind the guards came a small army of cleaning droids and gardeners to make sure everything was perfect for guests.

They had one argument about the throne itself.

"You want to tear apart a priceless antique and plant a blaster in it?" Amidala demanded.

The corridor outside her suite was not really the place for this argument, but Padmé had been so annoyed when she read the listed item that she barged out into the hall to talk to him about it. Padmé was not overly worried. It wasn't like anyone on this floor was unaware of her stance on taking arms.

"I won't tear it apart," Panaka said. "I was going to let Eirtaé do it. She's your engineer, after all, and she probably wants a challenge."

Eirtaé had spent the better part of a month engineering the Queen's new wardrobe to be as functional as it was osten-tatious, and if the number of sketches crowding the desk in the sitting room was any indication, she was hardly bored.

"And the blaster?" Padmé said.

"It'll be a small model," Panaka said. "Just a little power cell. And only for emergencies. If you're going to have foreign dignitaries in there with you, I want you prepared for the absolute worst."

Padmé leaned back against the window and sighed. Sanandrassa hadn't admitted very many offworlders to the throne room, and none of them had been violent. Surely no one would be so offended by two years of relative silence from Naboo's monarch that they would attack her in her own throne room. Yet Panaka was usually open to modifying his plans, if they discussed them with him. Over Panaka's shoulder, she could see Sabé. Her face was carefully neutral.

"It wouldn't hurt to expand your experience with weapons, Your Highness," Sabé said carefully. It sounded like she was awarding the point to Panaka, which was not quite what she was doing.

Whenever Padmé complained that she felt pushed into a corner by the demands of her guards, court, or colleagues, Rabé would remind her that it was easier in the long run to agree now and then press her advantage later. If they let Panaka have this, then Eirtaé would design something Padmé approved of, and Panaka would still think he had won. This was how Sabé reminded her of that. It wasn't a particularly subtle code, but the words they used were different every time, and so far, it had worked well enough.

"What if there were two blasters?" Padmé asked. Panaka

was clearly surprised. "I mean, if I'm the only one who has one, there's not much point. If we're going to arm one person, we might as well arm two."

"I can make it work with two," Eirtaé said.

"I like it," Panaka said, and it was decided.

"Very well, Captain," Padmé said. "Eirtaé will have designs to you the day after tomorrow. Do you have anything else that needs to be done this evening?"

"No, Your Highness," Panaka said. "Thank you."

Padmé went back into the suite and sank with a huff into a chair in the sitting room as soon as the door was closed.

"Even if we never use it, I'll always know it's there," Padmé said. "I'll always know that we think we might have to be scared of our neighbors."

"You'll be the only one who can open it," Eirtaé promised. That was something, at least. No one was going to break the blasters out willy-nilly. "And I'll make sure I don't ruin the throne."

"Thanks," said Padmé drily. She let Yané and Saché take her headpiece off now that they were in for the night, and accepted the facecloth from Rabé to clean her makeup off.

"The advisors are coming around," Saché reported when she returned from the dressing room. "Several of them were asked about the summit after the legislative session today, and they all managed to answer without looking like they disapprove."

"I guess there's a reason Bibble keeps getting elected," Rabé commented.

They watched Eirtaé sketch the blaster cabinets and listened to her talk out loud about her plans until Sabé began to second-guess them, and the conversation turned snarky.

"Just let me build a prototype before you dismiss it completely," Eirtaé finally said. "You're missing the whole point, and honestly, I'm starting to think you're doing it on purpose."

Sabé opened her mouth to make a reply, and then shut it firmly when she saw Padmé's expression.

"Can you pick nonmechanical locks, Rabé?" she asked instead. Everyone breathed a sigh of relief.

"Well, it's closer to slicing than picking," said Rabé. "But of course I can."

There were nonmechanical locks on several of Amidala's jewelry boxes, so Rabé and Yané fetched them from the dressing room, and they all took turns trying to break in without destroying the box.

"At least we didn't have to ask Panaka for these," Saché said, laughing gleefully as she finally cracked a lock open on her own.

"I imagine he'd have a few questions, yes," Rabé agreed. "Now see if you can do it in less than two minutes."

It took another hour before their times were consistently within Rabé's targets, and by then, Eirtaé had almost finished building a scale model of the throne with the modifications she wanted to add to the real one. Sabé tested the problem she thought she had identified, and found it didn't exist.

"You changed it," she said.

"Of course I did," Eirtaé told her. "Just because I still don't think it was a weakness doesn't mean I'm going to let it pass."

"You could have said something!" Sabé said.

"And miss the expression on your face right now?" Eirtaé replied. "I don't think so."

"This is why Panaka thinks he's aged ten years since the election," Saché said. "This right here."

"Here's to the next ten, I guess," Eirtaé said, lifting her teacup in a toast.

"And the ten after that," said Sabé.

DISTRACTION

ア1ハ↓7ㄷ'ㅓ↓1ㅇʌ

Eirtama had planned every part of the day down to the last detail, and it was not at all her fault that everything went wrong. She'd built the hoverpod based on her own designs, which she had created as an homage (no, she had not stolen them) to a piece used in the first opera that former Queen Réillata had starred in after her term. She was working with a much more limited budget, of course, and she had to do the whole thing by herself because her parents had sent her to a workshop for actors, which was not at all the same thing as a workshop for stage production, which had been her request.

Her parents were very good at almost getting it.

The opera was a slightly updated piece about the end days of human–Gungan conflicts, the sort of play old people liked because it made them feel safe, which made them willing to donate money to productions put on by students, who universally hated it. The pod was used to represent a sando aqua monster, from whose back the main character attempted to rally Naboo's tiny naval forces. Eirtama had designed the repulsor lift to accommodate four people. She had been very clear about the weight restrictions. And she had been ignored.

When the fourth soprano stepped up onto the hoverpod, it wobbled a bit alarmingly. But it held steady. In the audience, Eirtama had relaxed. This was going to be amazing. Surely someone would spend enough time looking at the singers to notice that what they stood on was a masterpiece.

Then a fifth soprano entered from the wings and began her ascent.

"Oh no," Eirtama said. The old woman sitting to her left shushed her quite loudly.

The music began, sound filling the concert hall as the audience prepared itself to be transported to an iconic time in Naboo history that had absolutely not happened. The set piece wobbled again.

"No," Eirtama said more loudly.

The old woman shushed her again, this time with an elbow to the ribs. Eirtama was pretty sure she was the lead tenor's relative. He was similarly intolerable.

"No, you don't understand," Eirtama tried to explain. "The pod isn't—"

Before the old woman could shush her a third time, or inflict bodily harm with her elbow, the loud buzz of an overtapped motivator sounded above the orchestra. One of the sopranos hit a note far, far higher than called for by the score as the pod careened wildly across the stage, bucking one of the singers off.

If that had been everything that happened, Eirtama would have called it a win. Sopranos were mostly insufferable. But she knew it was going to be worse. The sensors under the lift detected the fallen soprano, and the emergency override killed the repulsors, initiating the only safety protocol Eirtama's budget had allowed.

"Look out!" she shouted, because she couldn't think of anything else to say. It wasn't like ducking would help.

With a clash of metal and several more screams, the pod jerked backward into the rear wall of the theater, the only place guaranteed to be empty. The other four sopranos were indecorously dumped. Stagehands, most of whom considered themselves actors and were therefore wildly indifferent to the role, were quick to rush out to the fallen singers, but once they were there, none of them knew what to do.

A man with dark skin and a strong set to his shoulders pushed his way to the front of the crowd. He cupped his hands around his mouth, in too much of a hurry to identify the acoustic spots on the stage.

"Everyone remain calm!" he called out. "I am a trained professional, and I have already called for more help. Please exit the auditorium in an orderly fashion. If you are related to one of those injured, please come forward and make yourself known to the medics when they arrive."

Everyone did exactly what he said. Except Eirtama, who pressed forward despite not being anyone's relative.

"What are you doing?" He caught her by her collar as she tried to sneak past. Her blond hair spilled around his fingers, and she tried to wiggle free.

"I built it," she said. "I built it, and I was very clear that only four people should stand on it, and I will not let anyone say this was my fault."

He let her go, and she pulled her tunic back into place.

"Um, are they okay?" she asked. Most people would expect her to be friends with the people she'd spent a week workshopping a famous-if-slightly-problematic opera with.

"They're going to be fine," he said. "Maybe a sprained ankle or two at most, but no one broke anything."

"Except my hoverpod," Eirtama grumbled, then thought better of it. "I mean, I guess that's good."

"There's no shame in being upset when your craftsmanship is ruined because your advice has been ignored," he told her. "I think you're handling it pretty well."

The medics arrived, and Eirtama let herself drift out of the auditorium. She was now relatively sure no one would blame this catastrophe on her. She went back to the dormitory and read until she fell asleep.

The next morning, no one was entirely sure what to do. They were supposed to be striking the set, their grand performance done, but the set had literally struck itself. Instead, they milled around in one of the green areas outside the auditorium, waiting for instructions. No one waited with Eirtama. She didn't mind.

"Eirtama Ballory," a familiar voice called.

She looked up, and beside the director was the man from last night, the one who had called for help and kept everyone in the room from falling to pieces. The one who had believed her. Silence fell over the garden. Eirtama made her way forward. She was sure he had believed her. He had even told her she was handling it well. No one ever told her she was handling it well. She always overreacted.

"We met briefly last night," he reminded her.

"Oh, yes," she said. "The security officer."

His face twitched ever so slightly.

"I was very impressed with the way you handled everything, but I didn't get a chance to introduce myself," he continued. The last bit of her worry evaporated. "My name is Quarsh Panaka."

CHAPTER 11

The governor of Karlinus was the first arrival. Amidala met her at the landing pad as a sign of welcome and respect. Governor Bibble stood beside her, as he had met his counterpart before. She had only recently been elected, and Padmé hoped that she wasn't as soured to Naboo's recent policy as the rest of her government appeared to be. At one time, movement of people between Naboo and Karlinus had been quite common: Karlinus was a good place for artists to make money working the silk and tea harvests, and Naboo was a good place to set up a studio once an artist had acquired a bit of a nest egg.

"Governor Kelma," Amidala said as soon as she reached the bottom of the ramp. "Welcome to Naboo. We are pleased you were able to come."

Kelma extended her hand, and Amidala took it immediately. She could imagine the expression on Panaka's face, but she had told him that she was going to do what she could to make her guests feel welcome, and if that included handshakes, then that's what she would do.

"It was a surprising invitation," Kelma said. Her dark eyes

sparkled with amusement and her warm brown skin shone in the Naboo sunlight. "I was more than a little curious."

"I hope we can satisfy that curiosity," Bibble said magnanimously. He offered her his arm and chatted with her as they went back to the palace.

Kelma's eyes were everywhere as they walked, taking in every detail. She hadn't been to Naboo before, which was not an uncommon trait in their invitees, and she seemed determined to make the most of it. She wore a simple outfit for traveling: loose trousers under a tunic, all in matching linen. It was simple and elegant, and infinitely more comfortable than the dress Padmé was wearing. She was a bit jealous. She was also jealous that the governor didn't wear a wig. Her hair was thick and frizzy, which only made her round face seem more likable.

Karlinus was the only planet whose delegation Padmé met at the landing area. She had worried it would be viewed as a snub, but Bibble assured her that the other parties would understand that she couldn't run back and forth to the platforms all day. And in any case, several of them had been slightly rude in their responses, which meant that Padmé was allowed to be a bit distant until they warmed up to her in person.

The Chommell sector had more than thirty planets and several thousand settled dependencies. Padmé had invited all of the primary governments, but most of them had declined the invitation. A few had elected to attend via holoprojection, and a few more had agreed to come in person. Padmé had hoped for a better showing, but Bibble seemed pleased with the turnout.

"These planets represent our allies and our detractors," he'd pointed out once they had the final list. "Having them all in one room with us is a good first step."

Jafan and Kreeling arrived together. The two planets weren't in the same system, so Padmé could only view their arrival as a sort of statement. Unlike Kelma, who had come in person along with three aides, the planetary directors had sent ambassadors they thought were a match for Padmé herself. Specifically, their own children. Padmé was not insulted in the least, although she was reasonably sure that was the intention. Dealing with adults could be very tiresome.

"My name is Harli Jafan," a tall, hairless humanoid girl with light blue skin and delicately webbed fingers introduced herself. "My father is the planetary director."

"And I'm Tobruna." This was from a short human boy with red hair and brown eyes. "My mother is in charge of the Kreeling refineries, which more or less puts her in charge of the planet."

Padmé knew all of that already, but they had to start somewhere. Jafan was a relatively new colony. They'd arrived in the sector some three hundred years ago, and they were still ruled by the family who established the colony. Kreeling was a mining world. There was better money in shipping refined ore, so there were also a lot of refineries there. Rumors circulated that the methods used to maintain order at those refineries were less than democratic, but Padmé couldn't afford to let prejudice color her perception of the delegates.

"Welcome to Naboo," she said.

Padmé repeated the welcome again an hour later for the representative from Behpour, an elderly gentleman with black skin and mischievous brown eyes who seemed to be very good friends with Bibble, and then again one last time for the representative from Chommell Minor, a woman the same age as Padmé's mother who seemed deeply uninterested in the summit she had traveled across the sector for.

As the afternoon progressed, Padmé had welcomed half a dozen other delegates, bringing the total number to twelve, including herself. Mariek Panaka, as the highest-ranking guard in the diplomatic wing, was in charge of delegate security. The palace staff had been thoroughly briefed on the requirements of the nonhuman delegates. There was something in the Kreelingi atmosphere that had a permanent effect on human vision, Padmé suddenly recalled. She was sure her staff had it covered and would have made the appropriate arrangements, but she also knew she'd have to confirm it for herself, or it was going to bug her.

Padmé wanted to slouch when the final representative left to go to their assigned quarters in the diplomatic wing, but instead she maintained her dignity and let herself be borne off to prepare for the state dinner.

"You did ask for this," Panaka said.

"I am aware," Padmé replied.

He didn't push it.

𝒥𝒱𝒱𝒱𝒳

The handmaidens had two hours to prepare for the state dinner, and Rabé fully intended to use all of that time. First, they all scrubbed down in the royal baths. Usually they took their time in there—it was one of the few places they never had to worry about politics—but tonight they were on a mission.

Yané had laid out shifts for all of them to put on when they were dry, and when they got to the dressing room, she passed out jade-green robes for everyone but Padmé. The Queen was directed to sit and not move until given permission, and Padmé complied with a laugh.

"That means your face, too," Rabé said, hovering close with foundation and a brush. "I'm not making a mistake because you're giggling."

Padmé laughed harder, but schooled her expression when Rabé started to look exasperated. She closed her eyes and let the wardrobe mistress do her work.

Yané was braiding everyone else's hair so that they could pin it under their hoods. By the time she was done, Rabé was finished with the Queen's face except for the red marks, and so she went to get dressed while Yané stepped in. She braided Padmé's hair tightly and pinned it all down on top of her head. Then she covered the pins with a layer of gel that would stop them—and the wig—from itching. She fit the headpiece on carefully, checking frequently to make sure everything was aligned properly before giving it one final light shove down to attach it firmly to the gel. It was a traditional look tonight: a wide arch of hair that matched Amidala's natural color and several long tresses down her back.

Eirtaé and Saché had finished laying out the dress. It was one of Eirtaé's designs, and could be stepped into. This made everything about hair and makeup easier, and Eirtaé had grumbled for a week that it was ridiculous that it had taken *this long* for that to be normal. The dress was a deep pink in a less stiff style than Amidala's court gowns. There were actual flounces involved, which made moving around a lot more fun than usual, and the neckline was less conservative than her usual outfits.

Padmé stepped into the dress and stood patiently while they fastened it to her. Eirtaé went around behind her and activated the inner layers of the dress so they would seal around her body. Padmé had learned very early not to breathe out as that was happening.

"Cheater," Eirtaé said with some fondness as she tightened

the last few ties and then pressed the seam on the back closed, rendering it effectively invisible.

Sabé had been working on everyone else's makeup. It was another trick Rabé had devised. When they made up Amidala, they also made up the handmaidens to look as much alike as possible. It was only feasible when there were hoods involved, otherwise Eirtaé was an obvious outlier, but aside from that it worked quite well. Padmé had walked past Panaka three times as a page before he'd identified her.

After several minutes of small adjustments, Rabé and Yané pronounced everyone ready, and they set out for the dining room. The handmaidens would be at the table tonight, interspersed with various government officials. It was a deliberate show of trust on Padmé's part. She was giving her guests the opportunity to figure out something that was very important to her. The only questions were who would make the intuitive leap, and what they would do with the information. If she was being completely honest, Padmé couldn't wait to find out.

ꓶꙮꙮꓤ

Queen Amidala's first state dinner after being elected to her throne went, by all accounts, quite well. She had given thoughtful consideration to the menu, making sure to highlight Naboo delicacies without overwhelming her guests with fish. Though it was a staple protein on Naboo, the other planets in the sector did not support much aquatic life, and she knew the texture could be off-putting. The seating arrangement had been adjusted at the last minute to put Bibble next to Olan Carrus of Behpour when their friendship became apparent. Even though that put Carrus near the foot of the table, he seemed to appreciate the gesture. Padmé sat at the head of the table with Governor Kelma on one side of her and Nitsa Tulin, the representative from Chommell Minor, on the other.

The other delegates were interspersed with the handmaidens apparently at random, but it was no accident that Saché was seated with a clear view of Tobruna's and Tulin's faces. Padmé trusted her observations a great deal. Sabé was next to Harli, who turned out to be much more gregarious than any of them had anticipated. As the meal progressed, it was Harli who kept the conversation going, moving seamlessly from topic to topic. It was wonderful to watch, and it took a tremendous weight off of Padmé's shoulders, because she wasn't sure if Amidala was going to be a good dinner host.

"—and then the whole herd turned, and it was just my idiot cousins and me in their path," Harli said, winding down a story about the annual silpath migration on Jafan.

"What did you do?" Sabé asked, fascinated.

"Well, there was a tree," Harli said. "And I shoved my cousins up into it as fast as I could before I climbed up, too.

It wasn't much of a tree. I swear, some of the silpath had antlers that were taller, but at least we weren't on the ground with their hooves."

Carrus asked a question about herd numbers and how that affected the Jafani diet, which nicely distracted everyone until they moved out onto the balcony while dessert was served, to mill around and view the waterlight display Padmé had commissioned.

Over that last course of the night, while Bibble held forth about various escapades he'd experienced on all of their planets, Padmé was not so distracted that she didn't notice Harli flirt shamelessly with Sabé. What surprised her was the degree to which Sabé flirted *back*. Nothing inappropriate, of course, and it was possible the adults thought they were just quietly getting to know each other while the grown-ups talked about something they thought was boring, but Padmé could see the truth. She didn't know if Sabé was pressing an advantage or if there was a genuine attraction, and she didn't know how in the world she was going to find out, not without pulling rank. Her relationships with her handmaidens were progressing so *well*. She hadn't seen this coming.

As the dishes were being cleared away, Sabé caught her eye. She gave nothing away, her face orchestra-blank, and Padmé repaid the favor by not putting into her eyes a question she wasn't sure she should ask. Then Harli said something and Sabé leaned closer to hear it, and the moment was over.

Tobruna drew Padmé into a discussion about grav-ball with a very enthusiastic Eirtaé.

Finally it was time to bid everyone good night. They would meet in the late morning the following day to begin the actual discussions, and Padmé was very much looking forward to it.

"Well," said Sabé once everything was put away and they were all tucked into their beds. "This is going to be more interesting than I thought."

CHAPTER 12

"I know we won't be able to the change the minds of everyone in the sector after a single set of meetings," Amidala said at the conclusion of her welcoming remarks. The soft light of the throne room sparkled on the blue and green sequins of her dress, but that and the jewels on her headpiece were her only ornamentation. "Still, I hope that we can find a place to start."

As Governor Kelma rose to give a response on behalf of the invited guests, Saché took in the throne room. Even though Naboo was technically the chief planet in the sector and the only one to elect a queen, today Amidala was sitting on a chair that matched everyone else's, and the gesture had not gone unnoticed. Nitsa Tulin still looked bored and was only barely paying attention, but both Harli and Tobruna were visibly pleased to see Amidala sitting at their level. The only person who was upset was Captain Panaka. There were, in actual fact, two blasters currently hidden in the armrest of the Naboo throne. Meanwhile, the throne itself was sitting in an anteroom, waiting for Padmé to require it again.

"I'm sorry, Captain," Amidala had said when he'd confronted her about it. "I didn't do it on purpose, I promise you. There were so many other things to organize, and the chairs seemed like such a good idea. I forgot about the blasters completely."

Panaka glared at Eirtaé, who had definitely remembered.

"Please don't do it again" was all he said.

"I will not," the Queen promised.

The first day's schedule had been decided long before the delegates arrived, and it was the simplest. They met mid-morning to allow the two representatives with hyper-lag some time to catch up, and after the welcoming remarks, each person would have a few minutes to address problems specific to their own homeworlds. Governor Bibble did not expect any surprises, but none of the handmaidens—who watched from their places standing behind the ring of seats—were quite as blasé. Harli had the floor to start off with.

"Your Highness, honored delegates, observers"—this last was directed straight to Sabé, who turned ever so slightly pink and bent her head forward so that her orange hood covered more of her face—"Jafan has been on its own for nearly three centuries now. We know that we are not as well established as Naboo, but there is no doubt that we have our own culture and our own traditions.

"Did you know, Your Highness, that there are over three thousand Jafani citizens on Naboo right now, present company excluded?" Padmé did know this, but understood why Harli would say it out loud. "Furthermore, almost all of those people are artists. We are bleeding culture, my friends, and it's all ending up here."

Harli went on, giving the specifics about the demographics and disciplines of the artists who were leaving the planet. The problem was not that Jafan had no interest in its own culture, but rather that Naboo had similar interests, as well as more potential consumers. It was, put simply, more lucrative to be a Jafani artist on Naboo than it was to stay at home.

"Please correct me if I am wrong," Amidala said when Harli had taken her seat again. "But it sounds like this is a matter of accessibility and trade. If we can make it easier for people and works of art to move between planets, would that help?"

"It would be a start," Harli said. "Unfortunately, most forms of Jafani art aren't exactly portable."

Padmé remembered something about chalk scrapings on hillsides and vast rock structures that could be seen from low orbit. Landowners could commission the work, and then the Jafani artists would incorporate the landscape to make dramatic statement pieces.

"Of course," she said. "My apologies. Perhaps some sort of exchange program?"

"You did say we couldn't fix everything today," Harli said. "And I don't expect you to. In addition to the practicalities of it, there's a fair amount of prejudice between our planets, and all the cultural exchanges in the quadrant aren't going to make that any easier for some people to swallow."

"Do you think if we became regular trading partners for, say, grain and what have you, our people would get used to the idea of working together?" Bibble asked.

Padmé did her best not to wince. For a career politician, Bibble could be remarkably unsubtle sometimes. It was a large part of his charm and a reason so many people trusted him, but it still caught her off guard every now and then.

"Well played, Governor," Harli said, a smile on her face. "I suppose I walked straight into that one. It's possible. I am not sure how easy it would be to convince the director to part with food, though. It's been three hundred years, but we still keep very close stock of our supplies."

The floor passed to the next delegate, and talks continued. Nitsa Tulin passed on her turn to speak, and Olan Carrus said he had nothing to add. His planet's population was quite small, he admitted, and he had mostly come so that his government would have an accurate report about what had happened at the summit. Padmé accepted that with aplomb, and then it was Tobruna's turn to speak.

"Kreeling's problems are of a slightly more serious nature, I'm afraid," he began. "While we understand that the sector is famous for creation above all other things, it is we who are charged with the production of a key raw material.

An outdated treaty requires us to sell to Naboo and the other planets in the sector first at a fixed price, which means they always get the highest-quality ores at below-market prices. By the time our merchants are able to go out into the galaxy, they only have inferior material left."

They all had to be very careful with their answers to this one. It was one thing to promise support for a community of artists and another entirely to speak quickly of a planet's primary economic means, even at this early stage when no one was making any official promises.

"I know why you hesitate, Your Highness," Tobruna said. "We watched the election coverage, and we know that you pride yourself on your compassion. I know that you would like to offer the easy solution immediately, and I will not press you for any trade proposals today, or even tomorrow."

"We appreciate your understanding, and your generous read of our character," she said. "You are correct. We thank you for the time to consider our response."

Tobruna bowed and took his seat. This gave Padmé a few more moments to think about what she was going to say.

"Is Naboo your primary market?" she asked. "And do we require all of your high-quality ore?"

"You are," Tobruna said.

"We use the ore for shipbuilding," Bibble said, consulting his notes. "Most of it, anyway. The rest goes to musical instrument manufacture."

"Does that require high quality?" Amidala asked.

No one knew, and so Padmé risked a look at Sabé. They made eye contact, and Sabé minutely shook her head.

"One of my companions is an accomplished hallikset player," Amidala said. "Sabé, can you tell us?"

"Your Highness." Sabé bent slightly at the knee. It was the first time Padmé had ever called on a handmaiden for advice when they were in company. "From my experience, the high-quality ore is not necessary. The glint of the ore is fashionable, but not required."

Yané coughed quietly and adjusted her hood over her face before returning her hand to her side. Padmé remembered that within days of her handmaidens appearing in court with their heads covered, the particular handmaiden style had become a planetwide trend.

"That might not actually be so hard to change," Amidala said. "Especially if we convince up-and-coming musicians that a less glinty instrument is favored by the palace."

Tobruna grinned.

"I would not have thought of that," he said. "I look forward to seeing your solutions to the pricing issues, if they will be similarly creative."

"It is only a very preliminary stance, of course," Amidala said. "But we must all start from somewhere."

Governor Kelma had the last spot this morning.

"I know Naboo is facing its own labor shortage," she

began, "but Karlinus is in similar straits. We have plenty of people coming in to do the regular, year-round work, but it's the seasonal jobs that are suffering. They pay just as well, but it's hard to convince someone to move all the way out here if you can't promise them regular work.

"The people we want to hire from Naboo are ones you wouldn't miss, Your Highness," Kelma continued. "They're the young students right out of school who haven't decided which apprenticeship they want to take or what craft they want to dedicate themselves to. And we could use them. They'd be well paid, and when they returned, they'd be able to set themselves up pretty much any way they wanted to."

"My mother did that on Karlinus," Padmé mused. It had actually been Sola, her sister, but there were few enough students who made the trip now that if she'd specified a young person, someone might figure out who she was. "She always speaks highly of it. I know it was a good tradition, and I hope we can resurrect it."

"If you can," Kelma said, "then we can talk about grain."

Padmé nodded, and Bibble took that as his cue to end proceedings for the day. As she suspected, they had solved almost nothing, but at least they were all talking, which was the start she had hoped for.

"It was amazing to watch, Senator." Panaka hadn't been expecting Palpatine's call, but when the senator surprised him early in the evening on the first day of the summit, he was more than happy to take the call. "To watch her talk with the others and really listen. And make progress! Even if it was only the very beginning of mending the fences. Her handmaidens even offered advice."

"What an amazing accomplishment," Palpatine said. "I hope she didn't get too dramatic and promise them voting rights in the next election."

Panaka laughed.

"You know, I get the feeling she respects their sovereignty too much to do that," he said. "That's what made her so effective, I think. She wasn't the Queen today. She was simply their host."

"A united Chommell sector would be a force to be reckoned with," Palpatine mused. "There are several things I would like to do myself, but I find my hands are full representing the sector away from home."

"If the Queen has her way, you won't have to wait very long," Panaka said. He realized that he had been talking about the summit for quite some time, and that Palpatine was a busy person. "I'm sorry, Senator. Was there a reason you called?"

"No, not really," Palpatine said. "Just taking a moment to check in with an old friend. I am glad I contacted you, though. Such unexpected and thrilling news from home."

Panaka yawned, not quite able to hide it behind his glove. He'd called up extra guards, but he had still been awake for most of the time since the delegates had arrived.

"I won't keep you from your rest, Captain," Palpatine said. "I'm glad everything is going well."

"Thank you, Senator," Panaka said, and Palpatine ended the call.

$$\text{⟩⟨⟩⟨⟩⟨}$$

Darth Sidious considered his options. The events in the Chommell sector were completely unexpected. He hadn't thought that Queen Amidala could muster that sort of achievement in the short time since her election. It would be the last time he underestimated her. Even if she succeeded in uniting the system, he could still play it to his advantage. Ore traders and silpath hunters were no more a match for the dark side than Amidala was herself. He would have to move his timeline along, though. No more dallying on the Senate floor waiting for bills to pass. He would move the pieces directly, and if it cost him a few pawns in the process, well, he had plenty more where those came from. It was time for the Trade Federation to cease their training maneuvers, move their invasion force out of the wilds of Geonosis, and go to work.

CHAPTER 13

Sabé did not return to the suite with the Queen when she left the throne room on the second day of the summit. There was no formal dinner that night, so no one needed to prepare for anything. Padmé was looking forward to a quiet evening in her sitting room, discussing everyone's impressions of the day's talks. Sabé's absence didn't prevent her from dressing in more comfortable handmaiden-style robes and settling in with her tea, but Padmé found quickly that she missed her company. The others tried to distract her.

It was almost half an hour before Sabé let herself in. She was a bit breathless, like she'd walked quickly to come back to the room. Or maybe for another reason, but that was none of Padmé's business.

"Did you get lost in the corridors?" Rabé asked sweetly.

"Shut up," Sabé said. She looked to Padmé for support, but Padmé refused to meet her gaze.

"It's very good of you to pay so much attention to *relations*," Eirtaé said. Yané blushed and Saché looked uncomfortable. She'd been fighting a stomachache all day and wasn't in the mood for high spirits.

"You want to be nice to me," Sabé said. "I have an opportunity for us."

That got everyone's attention.

"Neurotransmitter Affection are playing in the Theed Odeon tonight," Sabé said. "One of Harli's cousins sings backup with them, so she can get us in."

Eirtaé made an unintelligible noise of excitement and Yané clapped a hand over her mouth.

"Harli Jafan invited us to a concert?" Padmé asked.

"Well, sort of," Sabé said. "She invited me. Unofficially. But she said that the rest of us could come, too. I imagine she meant the handmaidens, not the Queen, but there's no reason why a palace page can't tag along."

"Out of the question," Padmé said. "There's no way we'd even make it out the door, much less out of the palace."

"Don't be so quick to say that," Rabé said. "We haven't even started scheming yet. I am sure we can come up with something."

"What if there's an emergency?" Padmé said.

"Then we'll deal with it," Sabé told her. "Unless you don't want to go. It would be much easier to plan without you."

That lit a fire under Padmé's heart.

"I am definitely coming with you if you go," she said.

"I'll stay here, if that makes a difference," Saché said. "I don't feel very well anyway, and I've never been a fan of loud noises and crowds."

"We'll bring you back a souvenir," Sabé promised grandly. "Now, suggestions?"

Padmé listened to them plot, feeling strangely disconnected. Yes, Neurotransmitter Affection were shatteringly popular, but there was no reason to be so reckless as to go and see them. Unless Sabé really did like Harli. If so, Sabé would have to keep secrets from both, and surely that wouldn't be any fun. Unless she ended up liking Harli *more*. Padmé refused to go down that road. There was no reason to be jealous or doubt Sabé's loyalty. They were just going to a concert, like normal girls. One night. They could make that work.

Rabé shot down four suggestions before they hit on something she thought was feasible. Sabé, Yané, and Eirtaé would go to the concert with Harli, leaving in full view of the guards from the front of the palace. They wouldn't wear handmaiden robes, but they would be dressed as nondescriptly as possible. Meanwhile, Rabé and Padmé would go to the Queen's library, ostensibly to do research at Amidala's request. The guards wouldn't bother them, and Rabé would belay Padmé down the wall before climbing down herself.

"How will we get back in?" Padmé asked. There was no point in a one-way trip.

"I'll climb the wall and pull you up," Rabé said.

"It's five stories!" Yané protested.

"Do you have a better idea?" Rabé said.

Yané went over to one of the drawers on the side of the room and rummaged through it for a few minutes.

"Captain Panaka was annoyed that you wouldn't let him station guards in here, so he took steps," she said. She held up a grappling cable triumphantly. "See? Much easier than climbing."

"He's going to kill us," Padmé predicted. "But I'm not going to let that stop me."

They got dressed. It was fun to do more than one hairstyle, and Padmé was glad not to have the usual tight braids under a wig. Eirtaé took the time to curl her hair, since she only rarely got to show it off. Rabé and Padmé put on robes over their outfits, Rabé concealing the grappling cable under her skirt. They each took a few credits from Padmé's petty cash, in case of emergency, and folded them into various pockets—in Sabé's case, her boots.

Before they left, they made sure Saché was as comfortable as possible. She was curled up alone in Padmé's bed, feeling desolate and also too wretched to move.

"If your stomach still hurts in the morning, we'll call a med-droid," Yané said, brushing her hair off her face. Saché didn't flinch away from her, which was new. "It can't be food poisoning. You're not throwing up, and we all ate the same things."

"You should get going," Saché said. "I know Neurotransmitter Affection always have an amazing opening light show."

The three obvious concert attendees headed out. Padmé could hear them laughing with the guards in the hallway—this was the first time since their arrival at the palace that the handmaidens had worn nonmatching outfits, and it might be the first time anyone was able to immediately tell them apart. Rabé made them wait fifteen minutes, and then she and "Saché" headed for the library.

"How come they get to go to a concert and you two get stuck here reading up on ore processing?" one of the guards asked when Rabé explained where they were headed.

"Oh, we stayed home on purpose," Rabé said. "Neither of us really cares for crowds. A quiet night reading is much more our style."

The guard shook her head, but let them pass with no further questioning. Padmé kept her head down and hoped no one noticed that she was a solid five centimeters taller than Saché was.

Once they were in the library, Rabé stripped off her handmaiden robes and folded them roughly. Padmé followed a bit more slowly, also placing her robes on a chair in the corner of the room. Rabé opened the window and fired the cable up into the lintel.

"That will hold us both," she said. "You'll have to step on the ledge and put your arms around me, and then I'll lower us down."

"I thought you made and sold forgeries," Padmé said. "How do you know how to do all this?"

"Well, you can't forge something if you haven't seen it," Rabé said.

Padmé hadn't thought of it that way. She stepped up onto the ledge beside the ex-art thief and put her arms around her waist.

"Step with me on three," Rabé said. "One, two, three!"

Padmé leaned into her and took that first step into thin air. For a second, she was falling, and then the cable caught them. Rabé lowered them to the ground and pushed the retraction button. The cable detached and disappeared, and then Rabé stashed the grappler under a convenient shrub. She led the way through the gardens, whispering directions about how to make sure they stayed in the security system's blind spots. A quick scramble got her to the top of the garden wall, and she hauled Padmé up behind her.

"This is the hard part," Rabé admitted. "When you fall into the dry moat, make sure you bend your knees on the landing. And for the love of jogan fruit, don't bite your tongue."

Rabé slid to the edge of the wall and let herself down. Even hanging from her fingertips, she was a considerable distance from the ground. She rolled on the landing and came up quickly, brushing loose grass from her hands. Padmé did her best to duplicate the move, without the roll, and managed to knock the wind out of her chest when she landed. She sat gasping for a few moments, and then Rabé pulled her to her feet.

"Please teach me how to do that your way," she said when she had enough breath to speak.

"I'll put it on the list," Rabé said, grinning. "You did pretty well, though."

"Thanks," said Padmé.

The two girls hurried off. They were supposed to meet the others at the VIP entrance to the Odeon, and they didn't want to keep them waiting. It wasn't a long distance to cover, and there was a crowd to blend in with as soon as they reached the main thoroughfare. Padmé smiled in spite of her aching chest. She hadn't been around this many people in so long, and she had missed it.

Sabé waved them down by the entrance and introduced Padmé to Harli as a page that Rabé had stayed behind to escort.

"The more the merrier," Harli said. "Come on, let's go see what seats my cousin got for us."

𐤁𐤁𐤁𐤁

The seats were very close. And they weren't so much seats as they were places in the VIP dance area. This was entirely more than Yané had bargained for, and she was quite happy to stand at the edge of the dance floor and watch the stage. Eirtaé was deeply interested in the lighting design and had no wish to dance either. Rabé claimed to have two left feet, which Padmé highly doubted was true but didn't care enough about to argue.

Harli pulled Sabé out to dance as soon as the opening light show was over. The performers stepped into antigrav columns as the music changed and began to dance to the ironically titled "Get Down" while the audience did its best to emulate them on the floor. Sabé and Harli moved well together, and Padmé almost forgot to watch the band. She didn't like this feeling. She didn't think it was jealousy—not entirely, anyway. Before Harli had come, Padmé had known where she and Sabé stood. Sabé was the first of her handmaidens, the one who was the best at doubling for her and who would take the risks if there was any danger. And right now, Padmé didn't know how Sabé felt about any of those things anymore.

She should just ask. If they were normal girls, she would just ask. It was like those first few weeks when none of them had complained and just got more and more annoyed with each other. But they weren't normal. And while Padmé could ask as Sabé's friend, she wasn't sure if she should ask as Sabé's queen. No, she would have to wait for Sabé to come to her. And she didn't like that one bit.

The song changed, the tempo altering slightly but not

lessening very much as the solid sonic energy beams reinforced the beat. The lights all changed color and the crowd cheered as the stage was framed in streams of bright Naboo plasma. Sabé came over and grabbed Padmé by the hand, pulling her into the dancers. They moved together, and for a moment everything was the way it was supposed to be. Then Harli appeared at her elbow with a bunch of iridescent bulbs in her hands.

"They're glitter-lits," she said, yelling to make herself heard over the crowd. "Each section of the audience has a different frequency activation. I got some for all of us!"

Harli shook the lits to mix the chemicals together. She snapped one and handed it to Sabé. The main lights went out, and the Odeon thrummed with sound and color, but when Harli snapped the second one for Padmé, it broke and covered Padmé with glittering liquid that glowed in the dark.

"I'm so sorry!" Harli yelled. "But now at least you don't have to worry about holding on to anything!"

Padmé tried to brush the liquid off of her face and only succeeded in making a mess of her hands. Yané appeared with a scarf and a bottle of water, but even that wasn't enough to get rid of the stains entirely.

"We'll have to deal with it at home," Yané said directly into her ear. "Do you want to leave?"

"No," Padmé said. "We're all in this together, and I'm not going to ruin the night for everyone."

Yané looked concerned, so Padmé smiled brightly, and they both turned back to the show.

Every time Padmé caught sight of Sabé for the rest of the night, she was laughing.

CHAPTER 14

Panaka managed to have dinner with his wife for the first time in days. They squeezed it in right before she had to go on shift, and he wasn't able to do anything special on short notice, but at least they got to see each other. He told her as much as he could about the talks. The public transcript wouldn't be available for a few more days, but even working nights Mariek was bound to hear something via the palace gossip chain, and Panaka would rather she hear it from him. They were just about to dig in to the denta bean buns the kitchen had baked for the first day of the summit when Panaka's comm chimed with an alert he'd only ever heard once before.

After the Queen had refused to allow guards into her personal rooms, Panaka had taken some security measures he hadn't told her about. There was a weapons cache in the window seat, for example, which included a variety of things that would help the Queen escape or fight back if the occasion called for it. There were several sensors that could detect a perimeter breach, and several more for various types of weapons discharge. There was also a sensor that the Queen *did* know about, because one time Eirtaé had set it off when she was sewing and had pricked her finger with a needle. It was that alarm that was sounding now: the one that detected blood.

Mariek was on her feet before her husband was. She was already dressed for work, except for her jacket. She didn't stop for that as they headed for the door. Panaka didn't even stop for his shoes. She grabbed his shoulder as soon as they were in the barracks courtyard.

"Do not run," she whispered.

"I know," he muttered through gritted teeth. It was not as if anyone who saw him dressed like this would fail to be alarmed, but they had guests, and running through the palace corridors would attract too much attention. Padmé had the girls with her. He could be a professional.

They walked as quickly as they could.

The hallway outside the Queen's suite was quiet. The four guards on duty were standing at their posts. They jumped to attention when Panaka appeared, and when they saw his dishabille they went on alert. Panaka didn't stop to talk to them. He opened the door to the suite.

The rooms were empty and dark. Only a low light was on near the hearth. It was oddly calming, and Panaka did not wish to be calm. He had one priority, and that was Amidala.

He crashed into her bedroom, and the girl in the bed sat up and screamed.

⟨symbols⟩

Mariek followed Panaka into the Queen's bedroom. They both froze in their tracks at the scream, and Mariek turned to bring up the lights. In the center of the bed was Saché. She was pale and gasping for breath. They had scared her.

"Where is she?" Panaka roared.

Saché flinched back. She blinked, trying to wake up as quickly as she could.

Mariek put a hand on his shoulder.

"Let me do this one, love," she said. "Go and tell the guards in the hallway that there was no emergency."

Panaka obviously thought there *was* an emergency, given that the Queen was clearly not in her room, but he went anyway.

Mariek sat down on the edge of the bed.

"He's upset because the alarm called him away from a fresh denta bean bun," she said. Saché laughed at the idea that Captain Panaka ever chose dessert over duty. "It was the blood alarm, and I don't think it was a sewing accident this time."

Saché looked puzzled for a moment, and then connected the line between her cramps and the alarm. She looked under the covers and her face turned bright red.

"We keep the absorption pads in the bathroom," she said quietly, hoping the bed would swallow her whole. "The instructions are on the package. I can figure it out."

"I'll take care of the laundry," Mariek said.

Panaka was waiting for her in the hallway. He looked at the sheet she was carrying, considerably perplexed.

"Where do they keep their clothing?" she asked, as though everything was fine.

"What is going on? Where is the Queen?" he demanded.

"I haven't gotten that far yet," Mariek said. "You scared that poor girl half to death, and then mortification nearly took her the rest of the way. Just give us a few minutes."

Panaka watched while Mariek deposited the laundry and retrieved a clean set of bedding. She shuffled through the wardrobe registry until she found Saché's things, and called up fresh sleeping clothes for her. Then she carried them back into the Queen's bedroom. Panaka was on his last nerve.

"I'm assuming she's not injured, at least?" he asked.

"She's fine," Mariek said. "And you're an idiot for putting a blood-sensitive sensor in the bedroom of a teenage girl."

Panaka made several connections simultaneously, and had the decency to look guilty about it.

"It's never gone off before," he muttered.

"The older girls probably take suppressants," Mariek said. "You know, like literally every guard who cycles. We're busy people, Quarsh."

"I'll apologize for scaring her," he said. "As soon as she tells me where the Queen is."

Saché came out a few minutes later. She was wrapped in

a housecoat and looked incredibly embarrassed. She stared at Panaka's boots.

"There's a concert at the Odeon," she said, unprompted. "That's where they went."

"How did they get out?" Panaka demanded.

"Sabé, Yané, and Eirtaé left with Harli earlier." Saché paused. She didn't want to give up a secret, but there wasn't any way around it. "Rabé and Padmé left from the library."

"The library," Panaka said, extremely calm, "is on the fifth level of the palace."

"Yané found the grappling cable weeks ago," Saché said, gesturing to the window seat. "They used that."

Mariek made a noise suspiciously like a snort, and Panaka put his face in his hands.

"This is what we're going to do," he said after taking a moment to think about it. "We're not going to cause a scene. You're going to call the Queen and tell her to come home. She's going to come back the way she left so we don't make a spectacle of it."

"Okay," Saché said quietly.

"How is she disguised?" Mariek asked as the thought occurred. "If they're with Harli Jafan, she must have taken some precautions."

"They went as themselves," Saché said. "No one knows who they are. Tonight they're just girls."

"Call her, right now," Panaka said.

Saché fished the device out of her pocket and held it on her palm. At least the night couldn't get much worse.

ﾉᘜᘜᘜ

Padmé had her comlink in her pocket. She'd set the vibration as high as possible. There was no way she'd hear it over the noise of the concert, but she might be able to feel it. She wasn't really expecting anyone to contact her, but when the comlink shook against her leg, she knew there was only one person it could be.

She activated the device, and a miniature Saché appeared on her palm. Padmé couldn't hear over the noise of the concert, but Saché spoke clearly enough for Padmé to read her lips.

"Come home," she said. "We're blown."

Well. This was going to be fun.

Padmé got Rabé's attention. Rabé understood the situation immediately and went to corral the others. Sabé was still on the dance floor with Harli, so they didn't interrupt her.

"Padmé and I will go back," Rabé said when Padmé had caught them all up on the situation. "You two wait for Sabé and come back with her."

The trip back to the palace wasn't nearly as exciting as the escape had been. Panaka was giving them a chance to preserve their dignity, and the Queen's cover, and Rabé didn't waste it. She retrieved the grappling cable and got them through the window with no issues. They put their handmaiden robes back on and then went out to face the music.

The guards in the hallway were carefully neutral. None of them was exactly sure what was going on, and Padmé appreciated their discretion in not trying to find out now. Rabé opened the door to the suite, and they went in.

"We're in the sitting room," Saché called.

Padmé took a moment to pull herself together.

"Do *not* let him run over you," Rabé said under her breath.

"I won't let him run over *us*," Padmé replied.

When she went into the sitting room, she was dressed as a handmaiden, but she was Queen Amidala to her fingertips. Rabé followed a few steps behind, as though this were a normal walk in the palace, and instead of sitting down, she took a place behind Padmé.

"I don't even know where to start," Panaka said. He had gone through the heat of his anger and settled into a cold rage. He was doing everything he could to keep her safe, and she had all but thrown it in his face.

"We were given the opportunity to strengthen ties with the Jafani delegation," Padmé said. "I considered it an appropriate risk."

"Don't give me that, Your Highness." Panaka clung to his manners to keep from yelling at her. "You could have done that in the palace. You could have invited any entertainment you wanted. And instead, you slipped your guards, climbed five stories down, somehow got over the garden wall, and went out with no security at all!"

"Captain Panaka, you know that's not true," Padmé said. "You've trained my bodyguards yourself."

She used the word quite deliberately.

"It's not the same thing!" Panaka said.

"Yes, it is," Padmé said. For the first time, she unleashed the full brunt of her emotions on him: anger and frustration and a determination so solid, it would break rocks. "That was the whole point. They gave up their families and their names and their reputations, and they did it willingly, because they believe in your idea of what we could be. You trained us and gave us the ability to defend ourselves. We have worked to become a fluid, adaptable group, and we are powerful, Captain. Even if it's not the kind of power you are accustomed to."

Panaka sat back in surprise. And there was dead quiet for several moments.

"You are going to do things I don't like, Captain," Padmé said. "And I am going to do things you don't like. But at the end of the day, one of us was elected Queen of Naboo, and I will do my job the way I see fit. I will listen to your advice, the same way I listen to everyone, but sometimes I will act against what you've said. And you will have to do your job and protect me anyway."

"How can I protect you if I don't know where you are?" he asked.

"You gave me five protectors," Padmé said. "You'll have to trust them, too."

Panaka looked over her shoulder at Rabé, the girl he thought he could control. Her flat stare told him everything he needed to know. This was not a fight he would win.

"I understand, Your Highness," Panaka said. "Next time you want to go on an adventure, tell me first. I'll do everything I can to make it happen."

"I appreciate your dedication, Captain." She let him hear the affection, now, and the respect, since he'd gotten the negative emotions earlier.

"I'm late for my shift," Mariek said, admirably diffusing the tension. "And Saché probably wants to go back to bed."

She pulled her husband to his feet, and they took their leave. Rabé sat down and put her feet up on the little table.

"I ruined a bedsheet," said Saché, as though it made perfect sense. "And you are covered in glitter."

It was probably the adrenaline wearing off, but Padmé laughed until she cried.

CHAPTER 15

The glitter did not come off. Yané tried everything she could think of to wash Padmé's hands, but nothing worked. Eirtaé ran an analysis of the chemicals and tried to come up with a cleanser that wouldn't dissolve Padmé's skin off her bones, but so far she wasn't having any luck.

"Just try the makeup over it," Rabé suggested.

Yané went to work, but it was no use. The makeup they used as a concealer worked fine on Padmé's face, but cracked every time she moved her fingers. Yané tried a lighter application, but that wasn't enough to cover the glitter.

"It's daylight," Saché protested. "How is it still glowing?"

"It's a secret recipe," Eirtaé told her. "I had to slice into the manufacturer's database to find the ingredients."

"You can't go out like this," Yané said. "Harli will recognize you immediately."

"Gloves?" Rabé suggested.

"Not with a representative from Kreeling here," Yané told her. "It's not a rule, exactly, but it is a cultural guideline we should follow if we want to maintain our friendliness with Tobruna."

There was a whole moment where none of them panicked.

"It'll have to be Sabé, then," Eirtaé said. "She's the only one who has ever doubled for you in public, and her voice is the best. There will be quite a bit of speaking today."

Sabé looked up from where she was untangling strands of beads on one of the Queen's more ridiculous headpieces.

"What?" she said.

"Eirtaé's right," Padmé agreed. "You'll have to be the Queen today, and I'll watch the proceedings from the whisper gallery as a page. If I keep my hands in my sleeves, no one will see."

"This isn't tricking the guards or taking your place in a parade," Sabé said. "This is actual business. With serious ramifications."

"I am aware," Padmé said. Her voice was a little cold. "I knew when we went to the concert that there might be consequences, and here we are. Today, you're the Queen."

It served as a declaration, and the girls got to work.

Padmé and Sabé switched seats. The day's gown was quite formal. The rich burgundy was offset by light gray accents, and the headpiece was again the traditional fan shape. Rabé and Yané, who would accompany the Queen to the throne room, were in flame orange once more. It was quickly becoming their accepted color, and somehow the vibrancy of the fabric helped them to disappear. Saché helped Padmé and

Eirtaé into the muted blue and mercifully wide-sleeved robes, and they all secured their hoods.

"Thank goodness for fashion trends," Padmé said.

"Would you believe me if I said I wasn't surprised?" Yané asked.

"Yes," Padmé said, and meant it with her entire soul. "I would."

Sabé came over while Padmé was putting on the makeup that obscured her appearance.

"I'm sorry," she said.

"It's not your fault that the lit broke," Padmé told her.

"It's my fault you were there," Sabé said.

"I make my own choices, Your Highness," Padmé said. "You know that."

It sounded like they were talking it through, but Padmé had a feeling she'd only made it worse. There was no time for anything else, though. They all had places to be.

The whisper gallery was nearly full. The legislative assembly had stopped viewing the summit as a vanity project shortly after the first public transcript was released. Response from the general populace had been favorable, and now the elected officials were curious to see how everything turned out. Padmé and the others had seats in the reserved section as pages, which also meant anyone who needed a message run could call on them.

Two hours into closing talks, a representative caught Padmé's eye. There was no way she could pass the message to Saché or Eirtaé without raising eyebrows, so she got up and went to see what the message was.

"Please take this to the kitchen," the representative said. "We're leaving earlier than I thought, and I want to make sure the cooks have an accurate count for tonight."

For the first time, Padmé wondered why they didn't have a mechanized system for this sort of thing. It would not be difficult to send a brief message via comm, and while Padmé was perfectly capable of walking it down, she really didn't want to miss the summit. So much of Naboo's government was like that: a set of traditions that worked like Republic credits, valuable only because everyone had already agreed what they were worth. But that meant there were weak points to be exploited, and no defense against them. If Padmé didn't deliver the message, there would be an incorrect number of chairs at dinner. It wasn't a huge problem, but she was starting to wonder how else the system could be pushed.

Padmé committed the representative's message to memory and then exited the whisper gallery. She would come back as soon as she could. Since she was out of earshot, she was unaware that shortly after she left, Queen Amidala had called a brief recess, and she likewise hadn't seen Harli Jafan quietly excuse herself from the throne room.

Padmé was on her way back from the kitchen when she got caught.

"There you are!" said Harli, behind her and much too close. "When I didn't see you with the Queen this morning, I thought I was going to miss you entirely."

Padmé froze. She was wearing her own face, though her hood and the makeup obscured most of it. And this girl had come the closest of anyone so far to seeing through the Queen's disguise. She had counted the number of handmaidens in the room and realized Sabé wasn't among them. No one would think to look at the Queen, of course, but another robed girl in the palace corridor who was the same height was a logical guess. Particularly when that girl had deliberately taught herself to move the same way.

"I had a different job today." Padmé spoke as quietly as possible. Rabé said that quiet voices were easier to mistake. The Queen's voice had to be loud, so it required the most work. She turned so that she was half-facing Harli, but kept her head down and her hood low.

"I just wanted to tell you that I had an amazing time last night," Harli said. "I thought at first hanging out with your friends might spoil the mood, but they were so much fun, too."

"It was a good concert," Padmé said. She had never felt so exposed in her entire life.

"Are you okay?" Harli asked. "Did you get in trouble?"

"Captain Panaka is a worrier," Padmé admitted.

Harli laughed, and then reached out and took Padmé's elbows. She moved too fast for Padmé to dodge, and pulled her a little too close.

"Look, I'm not very good at this, and I know we literally live on different planets, but I like you a lot," Harli said. Padmé's heart raced, and not in the way Harli probably intended. "I don't know that much about Naboo dating culture, but I would like to kiss you before I go."

"Oh no," said Padmé. It was reflexive and absolute and *cruel*. She regretted it immediately, but couldn't think of anything else to do. She pulled away.

"Oh," said Harli. She sounded surprised. "You won't even look at me today?"

"I'm sorry," Padmé said. "I'm delivering an important message."

She fled, leaving Harli standing alone in the corridor and wondering what had just happened.

The rest of the summit closing passed without incident, though Harli spoke very little. The Queen presided over a farewell tea directly after the final session, and then each delegate took their formal leave. They would be departing the following morning, but this was to be the last official event. The handmaidens returned to the suite and prepared to spend the evening relaxing after a busy week. The decoy maneuver had, as far as most of them knew, gone without a hitch, and they were all in the mood to celebrate.

Sabé didn't get a chance to check her personal comlink or talk privately to the others until late in the evening. Yané had taken care of her undressing, and the others had gone to bed. Sabé could tell that Padmé had something she wanted to discuss and assumed it was merely that the Queen wished to evaluate her performance that afternoon. When she finally had a moment to herself, Sabé read a note from Harli with confusion that quickly changed into anger when she realized what must have happened. She went into Padmé's room. Saché was tucked under the covers, but Padmé was still reading.

"I got the strangest message from Harli Jafan just now," Sabé said acidly. "And frankly, I'm surprised I didn't get even a slight heads-up from you."

Padmé stilled. She set the documents down, and gave Sabé her full attention.

"It seems she tried to say good-bye to me this afternoon," Sabé continued. Her rage simmered in her. Saché was awake, but unmoving. "And I was very rude."

Harli had used much more colorful language.

"She surprised me," Padmé said. Her calm was completely infuriating, not because of her control, but because Sabé knew she was tailoring her deportment to Sabé's response. She hated being handled. "I wasn't expecting to be mistaken for you. It's supposed to work the other way around."

"And so you had to be awful about it?" Sabé said. "You can charm a whole planet into loving you, but you can't take two seconds to consider her feelings?"

"Should I have let her kiss me?" Padmé said. Her tone grew heated. "Do you think she still would have thought I was you then? Don't you think she might have recognized me from the concert, since I'm still covered in glitter?"

"I don't know!" shouted Sabé. She was aware that the others were standing behind her and modulated her tone so that the guards wouldn't come bursting in. "I just thought for one second, you might have been able to think of someone besides yourself."

There was nothing she could have said to hurt Padmé more, and she knew it.

"I tried, Sabé," Padmé said after a horrible silence. "I saw that you liked her, and I didn't know what that meant. If I were only your friend, I could just ask you, but I'm your queen, too. I can't order you to tell me about your personal life, can I? I had to trust that you would come to me and tell me what I needed to know. And you didn't."

"Did you think I would give up secrets?" Sabé asked. "Do you really think so little of me?"

"No," Padmé said. "I think the world of you. But it's harder than I thought to be your friend and your ruler all at the same time, and I can't do that if you don't help me."

Sabé sat down on the bed. The others came in and joined them, Saché pulling her legs up to make more room on her side.

"You wanted a normal night," Padmé said. "And I tried to give it to you. I thought that meant page-me could come with you, but I think it might be better if we avoided that from now on."

"I was sad enough that Saché missed the concert," Sabé admitted. "If you hadn't come either, it would hardly have been worth it."

"I thought you wanted to spend more time with Harli," Padmé said.

"I did," Sabé said. "She's the first person who's ever liked me for being me. But that doesn't mean I didn't want to spend time with all of you, too. Outside of this damn room."

"Well we probably can't use the library as a way out anymore," Rabé said lightly. "I think Panaka might be on to us."

Sabé giggled in spite of herself. They hadn't really solved anything, but at least they had identified the problem. That was a place to start.

"You can go if you want," Padmé said. "I don't know what you'd say, but you can have the night off."

Sabé was grateful for the offer, but it was too late. And Harli had as much as said she didn't want to see her again.

"No," she said. "What's done is done."

"I am sorry," Padmé said. It was all she could do, and it was not enough.

"Saché, would you switch with me tonight?" Sabé asked. She half expected her to refuse. It would mean sharing with Yané.

"Just this once," Saché said quietly. Yané looked down at her hands. Tonight was going to be deeply uncomfortable for everyone, apparently.

"Thank you," Sabé said. She knew it was important not to fall asleep angry with Padmé, however much she might want to. She didn't want to talk about it, but maybe if they were in the same room, everything would work itself out on its own.

"Maybe we should go to the lake house now that the summit is done," Padmé said. "It's early in my reign to go on a retreat, but I feel like we've accomplished a lot this week and could use a break."

"I'll look into it tomorrow," Yané said. She yawned. "Midafternoon, at the earliest."

Everyone left, and Sabé crawled into the spot Saché had vacated.

"Did you really want to kiss her?" Padmé asked.

Sabé knew what she was doing, and why she was doing it, but she couldn't bring herself to mend the fence. She could do her job, but that was it for now.

"Not yet, please," she said. "I just want to talk about politics."

Padmé dutifully changed the subject.

BRAVERY
⊟7ᴋYᴍ7Ɐ

The loom made her feel better. There were several different mechanized versions to choose from, looms that did all of the work and looms that let you maintain some semblance of control, but Suyan liked the manual ones best. Without a computer to tell her if the tension was right, she had to pay close attention, and she liked the way the world closed in around her as she wove. It shut out the bustle of the market, for starters, and sometimes that level of noise could be aggravating.

It was blankets, today. Simple enough, but Suyan was taking her time. Each one had a different design. They were all headed to the Theed hospital eventually, but that was no reason not to enjoy the process. Suyan loved watching the fabric grow under her fingers as she built it out of yarn, and she never got tired of the ways she could use color to tell whatever story she wanted in the weft.

"Are these all yours?" someone said.

Suyan paused and looked up. She needed her eyes to weave, and she didn't entirely appreciate the interruption. It was late in the day, and she'd already made several good sales. She wanted to finish this blanket and cut it free before it got dark.

"I made them, yes," she said. "They're for the hospital."

"They're very nice." The speaker was a tall man with brown skin and square shoulders. "What are they made of?"

"It's a yarn I make myself," Suyan told him. "I spin it from various components, and the end result is a blanket that is light, warm, moisture-wicking."

If he noticed that she didn't give up any of the particulars, he paid the courtesy of respecting her ownership. Some people tried to get her to reveal the combinations, and though she didn't mind sharing, she wasn't going to give them up to just anyone.

"Can you make fabric for other situations?" he asked. "Waterproof? Or fireproof, maybe?"

"Yes," Suyan said without considering it for very long. She was young to be a master weaver, and she didn't have the official designation yet, but it was only a matter of time. She knew the extent of her talents. "But I am not sure how practical that would be in a blanket at the hospital. They have other methods of fire suppression."

"I wasn't talking about just blankets," he said. He was still feeling the fabric, and she could tell by his touch that he didn't actually know the quality of the craft at all. She had no problem with people appreciating things because they were pretty or soft, but his questions didn't link up with his behavior. "Can you only make heavy yarn do what you want?"

"The bulk makes it easier," she admitted. "But not everything has to be in the weave. There are resins that can be used to treat fabrics and still maintain their flexibility. And you could probably do a lot with embroidery, if you had the right sort of thread."

He considered it for a moment, and she thought he would keep walking. Instead, he returned to the red blanket she had finished that morning and hung up to make sure the blocking was all right.

"Do you always work here?" he asked, indicating the market in general.

"Sometimes I work at home," Suyan said.

"Sorry," he said. "I mean, are you always a weaver?"

"No," she said. "I have to spin my yarn, as I said, and I also dye it myself most of the time."

"Is that all you've ever wanted to do?"

It was an oddly direct question, and Suyan considered her answer before she gave it.

"Yes," she said. "I'm happy."

"Would you consider another job, if it became available?" he asked.

"Nothing ever has," Suyan said.

He looked straight at her, no longer running his hands along the blanket weave.

"It would be at the palace," he said. "There would be a lot of people. You wouldn't have very much time to yourself. It might be dangerous. And it's very important."

Suyan rested her hands on the top of the loom, letting the shuttles go and taking her feet off the pedals. She realized that whoever this man was, he definitely hadn't found her by accident. He hadn't been walking in the market and been attracted by the bright colors of her stall. He had known she would be here. He knew what she did. He had come here to ask her these questions, even though he knew most of the answers already. And he had done all of it on purpose.

"I'm a weaver," she said.

"You're an artist," he replied. It was a common designation on Naboo, but the way he said it gave it more weight than she was used to. "You have a very interesting skill set, and I am very interested in seeing you realize its full potential."

175

"*Weavers don't usually have dangerous jobs,*" she said. *Even dyeing cloth, which had been hot, heavy work before automation, was relatively safe as long as you didn't do anything stupid.*

"*There's another part to it,*" he admitted. "*You'd be responsible for the well-being of a high-ranking official, and I would expect you to use all of your skills to protect her.*"

"*You're Royal Security,*" she said, narrowing her eyes at him.

"*Captain Quarsh Panaka,*" he introduced himself. "*I'm head of Queen Amidala's guard detail.*"

The thing about weaving blankets for the hospital was that Suyan got the feeling of having done something good without really extending herself. Yes, it was fun to do the work, and yes, she enjoyed coming up with new fabric blends, but the truth was that she mostly did it because it made her comfortable. What Captain Panaka was describing sounded terrifying. Suyan did not have to be told the power of a good weave, a good thread, a good seam. She already knew those things. If anything, she wasn't used to that power being acknowledged.

She was less sure that she, Suyan, would be any good at protecting someone.

"*All right,*" she heard herself say. "*I'm in.*"

CHAPTER 16

Queen Amidala spent the morning on the landing platform, waving decorously as her guests departed. She was accompanied by a single handmaiden and a handful of guards. No one would have guessed it by looking at her, but Padmé was exhausted. At least the dress was doing most of the work for her, in terms of standing up straight.

Panaka was squinting up at the sky, a puzzled expression on his face.

"Captain?" said the Queen.

"We're getting some unexpected feedback on the outer signal buoys," he said. "Who is left?"

"Just Governor Kelma," Saché said. "She volunteered to go last because she has the least hyper-lag to worry about."

"I'm going to call her pilot and tell them to get a move on," Panaka said. "We're going to have to send some of our own ships out to check on the buoys."

"As you say, Captain," Padmé said.

The Karlini ship took off the moment its preflight checks were done. The comlink was still open, and as the ship cleared orbit, Padmé heard someone very clearly.

"What the hell?" was all that was discernible before the ship was out of range, but it was enough to raise Panaka's hackles even further.

"I'd like you to go back to the palace, Your Highness," he said.

Padmé did not consider arguing.

Saché had her comlink out and sent a short message to the others, who were hopefully still in the suite. They had dressed Padmé in another formal gown this morning, one that would be visible from a ship while she stood on the landing pad. The gown was red with a wide skirt and elaborate tabard that covered her shoulders and chest. Around the skirt was a ring of luminescent orange and yellow globes. It wasn't exactly a dress to move quickly in, but Padmé managed, even on the steps. At the door to the palace, Padmé stopped and turned to one of the guards.

"Would you please find Governor Bibble and ask him to come to the throne room?" she asked. Tradition or no, she was going to update the messaging system. "Captain Panaka has a report to give."

The wording was deceptively light, and Padmé could see that the guard understood her immediately. She set off at a trot, and Padmé continued toward the throne room. She had a bad feeling.

The personal comms in the Queen's suite all went off at the same time, which would have been alarming on its own. Four miniature versions of Saché appeared on four palms, and immediately their attention was riveted.

"Flame" was the only thing she said before she disappeared.

It was one of the first codes they had devised. Rather than have a single word that would call them all to action in case of an emergency, they had a few different ones to help indicate what sort of emergency it was. The color of the robes Saché had been wearing that morning—the ombré orange to yellow, in this case—meant that they all needed to appear as hand-maidens in the throne room, as soon as humanly possible.

They didn't bother to braid their hair. Instead, robes were thrown on and pulled straight, and everyone was left to tuck her hair in as best she could. Sabé led the way through the corridors at a fast walk. No one else seemed to be respond-ing, so Amidala still required their discretion. They reached the throne room doors and saw the Queen was already sit-ting, with Saché at her side. The rest of them hurried to their places.

"Governor Bibble, thank you," Amidala was saying as the governor entered from the other side of the room. "We know you meant to depart this morning, but Captain Panaka wished you to be present."

"Of course, Your Highness." Bibble was too practiced a politician to show his annoyance openly, but he could hardly be blamed for wanting to be elsewhere. He'd had a long week, too.

"Your Highness, Governor Bibble." Panaka strode into the room, his boots ringing on the marble, and stood in the center of the floor. "Just as Governor Kelma's ship was leaving orbit, our external buoys were buzzed by a small craft of unknown design. We assume they scanned us for planetary defenses, but everyone knows we have none. We do not know—"

A holo blurred over him, and he stepped aside to let the image clear. Even though he knew the person wasn't really there, he couldn't help reaching for his blaster.

"Your Highness," said the figure. "I am Viceroy Nute Gunray of the Trade Federation. I require you to sign a treaty."

"Viceroy, this is highly unorthodox," Amidala said. "We are not in the habit of signing treaties with people we have only just met."

"Nevertheless, you will sign this one," Gunray said. "It is being delivered to you as we speak."

Sabé went to the console and nodded. Whatever document the viceroy meant had appeared in the Queen's database. Her hand hovered over the disconnect switch, but she waited for the signal.

"We will have it added to our schedule," Amidala said, "and contact you in due time when full consideration has been given."

"You will sign it," Gunray said. "Or you will suffer."

He disappeared.

"Your Highness," began Panaka, but Padmé held up her hand.

"Captain," she said. "Please ready your guards and the rest of the Security Forces. I know we do not have much in the way of planetary defense, but I will not sit idly by until we have determined what this Viceroy Gunray is after.

"Governor." She turned to Bibble. "I am sorry, but I will need you to stay in the palace for a bit longer."

"It won't be a real treaty," Bibble said. "They expect you to capitulate without a fight."

"They expect incorrectly," Padmé said. "But there may be hints in the document as to what their game is. I recommend you and your staff read quickly."

"I will make arrangements," he said. He stood to go, but Padmé raised her hand again to stop him.

"Governor, who on Naboo is empowered to sign treaties with offworlders?" she asked. "I must confess, I am unfamiliar with the exact chain of precedence, and I would like that clarified as soon as possible."

"The Queen is the only person with that power," Bibble told her.

"And if the Queen is absent or incapacitated?"

"They must wait for her recovery or return."

"And if the Queen is dead?" She didn't flinch.

"Then there must be an election, Your Highness," Bibble said, his discomfort obvious in his tone and the way he twisted his hands. "It has never happened."

"Thank you, Governor," Padmé said. "We will reconvene in two hours."

ᑊᐯᐯᑊ

The treaty was, in Sio Bibble's professional opinion, a pile of shaak shit. Naboo would be indenturing itself to the Trade Federation's whims and stood to gain absolutely nothing from the arrangement. They couldn't possibly expect the Queen to sign it.

They must have some darker purpose. Bibble went through every note he could find about who had signatory power in case of emergency to see whether his original statement to the Queen had been incorrect. If the Trade Federation sought to install a puppet queen who would be more amenable to their demands, that would be another matter. Everything he found indicated the same thing: he'd been correct. Only the Queen could sign, nothing short of her death would change that, and even should the worst come to pass, nothing could happen until they had another election. Legally, they were going to be fine.

Bibble started to worry about all the less than legal ways that this could end poorly as he headed back to the throne room.

"I need to contact Senator Palpatine," Padmé said. "Use his emergency channel, if you can find it."

"If I can find it," muttered Eirtaé. Within seconds, she had set the comm up and ushered Padmé into the right place to stand for the holoemitter.

Whatever time it was on Coruscant, Palpatine must have been awake, because he answered her immediately.

"Queen Amidala?" he said, shimmering blue in front of her. "This is an unexpected surprise."

"I'm afraid I have bad news, Senator," Padmé said. "And no time for pleasantries."

"Oh dear." Palpatine sounded a little out of breath. Maybe he'd come running when he heard the emergency channel. "Please, go on."

"We received a threatening communication from Viceroy Nute Gunray of the Trade Federation," Padmé informed him. "He demanded that I sign a treaty. I refused, of course. And I will refuse again. We've had time to read it, and he's asking me to sign over the whole planet."

"I was afraid something like this might happen," Palpatine said. "But never in my wildest dreams did I think it actually would! Your Highness, the Trade Federation is behind a conspiracy in the Senate to shift the tax on trade routes, and Naboo is right in the middle of their proposed operation."

"We kept hearing that the bills had failed," Padmé said.

"They have," Palpatine said. "It looks like the Trade Federation is taking a more extreme approach."

"Captain Panaka and the other officers are taking what measures they can," Padmé said. "For now, there is nothing we can do but wait. I wanted to inform you in case you had any suggestions."

"I will take it to the chancellor," Palpatine said. "It's always best to go straight to the top."

"Thank you, Senator," Padmé said. "Now I'm afraid I must go."

"Be safe, Your Highness," Palpatine said. "You are far too important to lose."

Rabé cut the connection.

"It's time to go back to the throne room," she said.

"Are all of you all right?" Padmé asked before they set out again. "I know these past few days have been a lot."

"We're fine," Sabé answered for everyone. It was more or less the truth.

The door to the sitting room burst open and they all jumped.

"Your Highness," Panaka said. "The Trade Federation is here. In orbit. They've blockaded the planet."

Darth Sidious looked at the hologram of Naboo that hovered over his desk. It was a beautiful world. Clear waters and green trees, yellow stone and blue skies. People who wanted nothing from life other than to make pretty things that made other people happy.

He wanted to make sure its legacy was never forgotten.

And now he had the means. Orbiting the planet in a perfect circle were dozens of ring-shaped blockade ships. Each was heavily armed and even more heavily shielded. And all of them were packed with droids.

He'd been pleasantly surprised by the ingenuity the Geonosian engineers had shown in designing the invasion force. There were droids for every rank and every task, just like in a regular army. They would be able to overwhelm the Naboo completely, and they might not even damage the planet all that much. Not at first, anyway. Sidious preferred complete destruction, but desecration would do in a pinch. The hologram glowed, and he reached out to put a fingertip to where Theed would be, as if he could crush it.

The other console, the one in his public office, chimed loudly enough that he heard it through the closed door. It was probably Chancellor Valorum. Right on schedule.

CHAPTER 17

The first week under the Trade Federation blockade was both extremely tense and incredibly boring. Most of the time, there was nothing to do but wait. Padmé spent hours in the throne room with various government officials, theorizing how Naboo could defend itself and wondering which allies they could ask for help. Any communications they sent out were answered more than a little vaguely. There was no doubt that the Trade Federation was listening.

She was never without her handmaidens. At least two were beside her all the time, while the others cycled in and out of the room on various errands. She began to give them their own assignments, rather than waiting until they had retired for the evening and running a debrief as a group. It was not how the system was supposed to work, but they had to adapt.

She was no closer to patching things up with Sabé, but the other girl seemed to have pushed all emotion aside and thrown herself into her duties as though there was nothing else to be done. Padmé couldn't do anything but wait her out, too, even though all the waiting was starting to make her a bit short-tempered.

The viceroy refused to come down to the planet, nor would he send a live representative. He insisted that Amidala join him in his headquarters in one of the orbital ships, but that was obviously out of the question. Since she wouldn't cede to his demands, he began sending down droid emissaries, all of which carried a variation of the same message. Padmé returned every one of them, unanswered and unsigned.

No ship was allowed to enter or leave planetary atmosphere. The Naboo Royal Space Fighter Corps hadn't pressed the Trade Federation to see if they would actually shoot exiting vessels down. They had run a few drills in low atmosphere and received an automated warning from a droid not to fly too high, but they hadn't seen any enemy ships flying in formation. The stalemate made no one happy, but it was better than an all-out war.

On the seventh day of the blockade, an agricultural transport from Karlinus approached the orbital line. Governor Kelma had sent the shipment as a sign of good faith, a thank-you for reopening lines of communication between the two worlds. It was a relatively small amount of grain, but the symbolic gesture was unmistakable. The ship was refused passage and forced to divert to Enarc, where the cargo was put into cold storage. It was the first real test of the blockade, and the Trade Federation had won.

"How much of the crop did we actually harvest?" Amidala

asked her agricultural advisor, several hours after the standoff was over and they'd all accepted the ship wasn't coming.

"It's more complicated than that, Your Highness," Graf Zapalo said. "The first yield is always weaker, so we elected to turn most of it into fertilizer. We harvested maybe an eighth, and that has already been replanted for the second half of the growing season."

"So when the legislature decided on half, they meant the *second* half?" Amidala asked. She should have known that. There were too many details to keep straight.

"Such as it is, Your Highness," Zapalo said. "We were expecting the first shipment of offworld grain two days after the blockade was implemented, but it's from a planet allied with the Trade Federation, so we started looking elsewhere. The Karlini grain would have held us over, but it won't make a difference if nothing can get through."

"How much food do we have in reserve?" The Queen's voice made the question seem cold, which covered Padmé's rising concern.

"Onworld?" Zapalo paused to do some calculations. "We can support the city of Theed for a month."

"There's more to Naboo than the city of Theed," Amidala said, a gentle rebuke.

"Of course, Your Highness," he said. "If we are feeding the whole planet, our supplies would last a week. Each population base has their own storage facilities, but we would have to supplement them from the capital."

"You're saying we have enough food for a week?" Amidala asked. It seemed a very small amount of time.

"Public food, Your Highness," Zapalo said. "That doesn't take into account any food on the general market, or what the farmers have in their private stores."

Padmé was about to ask if there was a census of that sort of thing, but stopped herself. Either there was, and she should have already looked it up, or there wasn't, and she'd only make Zapalo look foolish when he had to admit it.

"Do you have an emergency plan for this sort of situation?" Amidala asked instead.

"By region, yes. But the response is tailored toward natural disaster, not foreign blockades. We don't have one plan for the entire planet at the same time," came the reply.

"Eirtaé will accompany you and help you draft one," Amidala said. "We want something we can implement by the end of the day."

The agricultural advisor looked like he wanted to protest, but Eirtaé gently guided him from the room.

"Has anything else changed?" Amidala asked.

"Chancellor Valorum's ambassadors should be here tomorrow," Bibble said. "His office indicated they will meet with the viceroy first, but with the blockade, that was probably inevitable anyway."

"We must put our faith in the ambassadors," Amidala said. "Yané, please inform the kitchen that we are switching to rations, starting as soon as possible. If we have to make an announcement to the general populace, we wish to be leading by example."

Yané curtseyed and left the room.

"I don't suppose you would consider going into hiding until all of this is over?" Panaka asked.

"No, Captain," Amidala said. "But as always, we appreciate your concern for our safety."

"It was worth a try," he said.

Padmé dressed for the chancellor's ambassadors with as much care as she might have under better circumstances. She wore the red dress with the wide skirt and shoulders again. It was the most wearable dress she had that was suitably regal, made so by careful design and potolli-fur trim. Yané had tweaked the outfit so that Padmé no longer required an underdress. She had just a jumpsuit on, and the dress supported itself. That made the outfit lighter and easier to move in. Yané did an impeccable job of her makeup, and by the time the headpiece slid on, the jewel of Zenda pressing against her forehead, Padmé was feeling almost confident.

They all trooped into the throne room to wait, and passed

the time by organizing ration plans. When two hours had gone by, Padmé sent a message to Nute Gunray, reminding him that she knew the ambassadors were due. The viceroy seemed too smug.

"Do you think Republic ambassadors would be susceptible to bribery?" she asked the room in general when the call was completed.

"I would hate to jump to conclusions," Bibble said. "But nothing is impossible."

"Contact Senator Palpatine," Padmé said. "Maybe he can at least tell us who was sent."

Senator Palpatine was available, but his image flickered out before they could have any real discussion. Bibble immediately declared what everyone was thinking: invasion was nigh. Panaka and the governor quibbled about how to respond, and before they could make any real decision, it was made for them: the Trade Federation ships were already landing.

It was not enough time to scramble their ships. The pilots in the Theed hangar were the first targets, and they lost contact with them immediately. The few ships that made it to the sky were shot down before they could do any damage. It was only a matter of time before troops reached the palace.

Panaka ordered them out of the throne room immediately: there were too many windows and it was not a good place to stage a defense.

"Governor, I recommend you go to your office," Panaka

said. "The palace guard will do what they can to secure you there. Your Highness, it's time to go."

Bibble looked terrified, but he went. Padmé followed her guards back up to the suite. She was so busy trying to calculate the exact amount of time it would take to breach the palace doors that she didn't realize why they were headed there until just before they arrived. Then she turned and caught Sabé's hand.

"Anything we have to sort out, we can do it later," Sabé said. "From this point on, I'm yours."

It was an incredible gift. Padmé didn't think she'd ever be able to swallow her pride like that, and she admired Sabé tremendously for it. This, she knew, was why Panaka had recruited her, but it was still remarkable to see.

The changeover would have to happen more quickly than they'd ever managed it. Sabé shed orange robes for a black dress, all of the handmaidens focusing on her for the time being. Alone for one last precious moment, Padmé drifted over to the window in the corridor. The guards gave her space to think. Face solemn, she looked out over the city, committing the architecture to memory even as the droid army marred it, and making silent promises she wasn't entirely sure she could keep.

Padmé wiped the Queen's face off before getting a set of robes for herself. She made sure the handmaidens looked to Sabé, not to her, for guidance. This was the real test—the first time they'd ever done it when there was real, personal danger involved.

Sabé led them out onto the terrace, bidding the guards to join them, and they waited for the inevitable.

Jar Jar Binks was having a terrible afternoon. Disaster had always plagued him, it was true, but today the galaxy seemed to be taking it to extremes.

The accident was definitely his fault. Usually the mayhem he caused was more a case of inadvertent bad luck, but this time he had *really* messed up. Forced to leave Otoh Gunga and too afraid to stay in the deep water by himself, Jar Jar made what he thought was a pretty clever move. He'd gone up to the surface. He'd scrabble out a living there, he decided, until Boss Nass's temper had cooled, and then he'd try going back. It was nothing a little time wouldn't fix. He'd just stay out of the way for a while.

He was not expecting his first week in above-water Naboo to include a fleet of ships descending to the planet's surface. The ships were ugly; there was no grace to their design at all. Instead, they were blocky and brown and altogether unpleasant.

Also, they deposited large hovering tanks that didn't watch where they were going and didn't care whom they crushed.

The upside was that someone rescued Jar Jar, and that

rescuer was a Jedi. Gungans were an insular people, but they knew what the Jedi were, and if there was going to be a mess on the surface, Jar Jar was in good company. The downside was that the Jedi and his apprentice wanted Jar Jar to take them to the underwater city, even though he'd only *just* been banished. They even had little breathing devices so that they could handle the depth with him.

And *then* they all ended up in the planet core. It was the worst day ever.

When the bubbles of the bongo popped open in the Theed estuary, Jar Jar didn't think he'd ever been so glad to see something that wasn't water. He'd heard stories about how uncivilized the Naboo were all his life, but the buildings he saw indicated that they must be at least reasonably intelligent. They were pretty enough, even though they were straight and domed instead of being fluid and curved, and there was even some art he thought wouldn't be too out of place in a Gungan exhibit. The only problem was that the city was covered in more of those ugly brown ships.

By the time they had gotten safely out of the water, they had to move carefully through the city to avoid droid patrols, which was not really something Jar Jar was very good at. He managed to keep his mishaps mostly small, only tripping once, and then into a very quiet pile of rugs. At last, they were in a small walkway over the street, and the Jedi named Qui-Gon called a halt.

"Down there," he said.

They looked carefully over the foliage and saw a strange procession. Several droids were escorting almost a dozen people dressed in various uniforms. In the middle was a short human female in a black dress and makeup Jar Jar would have recognized anywhere.

The Jedi leapt down to attack the droids, and Jar Jar Binks followed them, straight into the arms of his destiny.

CHAPTER 18

"We are brave, Your Highness."

The Jedi's choice was a hard one, and everything inside Padmé screamed to stay with their people. She wasn't entirely sure she trusted Qui-Gon Jinn yet, but she knew Panaka would probably get himself killed if they stayed, and Governor Bibble seemed to think that going to Palpatine was their best chance now that they'd been overrun, and Padmé agreed with him.

They couldn't all go on the ship. Space was full of hard limits that no amount of clever negotiation could cross. There was only a moment to choose who would stay and who would go, and Padmé didn't even get to make the final call. Everyone looked to the Queen, and Sabé declared they would go to Coruscant. Yané took Saché's hand and walked over to stand with Bibble. There wasn't even time for a proper good-bye. They had to get to the hangar, and then it was all blaster fire and carbon scoring until they were free of the blockade.

As Naboo disappeared behind them, neither Padmé nor Sabé could shake the feeling that they had only just begun to encounter things that were beyond their control.

The first thing the droids did was scan them. This was mostly painless, except for the small prick that accompanied the blood test, and then they were all shoved into a small house off the courtyard where they'd been captured.

"You will remain here until you have been designated," said the droid who seemed to be in charge. "Any attempt to escape will be met with violence."

Saché had no plans to escape.

She and Yané sat together. Several of the guards paced restlessly, but the girls were deep in their thoughts. Even now, the Queen was running the blockade, and they would have no real way of knowing if she'd been successful unless their enemies decided to tell them. After half an hour, a droid came with an order to remove Governor Bibble and take him back to the palace. He left alone, and Saché could only hope that he would be all right.

They waited another hour. Even the most restless of the guards stopped pacing and sat down. Yané moved closer, and for the first time, Saché didn't care. She wasn't alone, and even if her feelings were complicated, at least they would have each other. Finally, the door opened.

"On your feet, humans," said the droid. "Come with me."

They were marched through the center of Theed and into

the largest market square. Everything in the square had been flattened: the fountains, the benches, the statues. Usually the market hummed with life and commerce, but right now the only sounds were the clank of droid feet and assorted noises that accompanied the hasty erection of a small tent city.

"You have been designated for camp four," the droid informed them. "Prepare for incarceration."

They were escorted to one of the new tents and pushed through the flap. Inside were two rows of cots and what appeared to be a shared toilet at the back. A few guards were already waiting inside, and Saché was relieved to see Mariek Panaka among them. Mariek pushed her way toward them and looked closely at their faces.

"Did she get away?" she asked, her voice low.

"Two Jedi found us," Saché said quietly. "If they can't get her off planet, no one can."

Yané was examining the setup inside the tent with a critical expression. It was easy to tell that there weren't enough beds. She doubted the droids would be taking requisitions. The earliest Padmé could make it back was three days, and that was if everything went perfectly on the trip, in the Senate, and on the trip back. If she took much more than a week, they'd all be uncomfortably hungry and thirsty, unless the Trade Federation decided to do something to keep them alive. The perfect storm of Naboo's food shortage and the planetary blockade would get even worse if there was a water shortage as well. It was the hot season, and the camp was definitely overcrowded.

Mariek spoke quietly to a young guard with a wide face and dark hair. He nodded and went to the opening of the tent. It was clear he had been assigned to keep watch. Mariek gestured to the girls to come close. They had no idea how well the droids could hear.

"Report," Mariek said. She could tell Yané had been running logistics.

"We should be all right for a few days," Yané said. "Much longer, and food will be a major issue. I haven't located a water source yet, but there used to be four fountains in this market, so there must be something somewhere."

"That takes care of this tent," said a guard Saché didn't recognize. "What about the rest of them?"

"We'll do a survey once the building stops," Mariek said. "There's no point in taking inventory when the droids are still moving things around."

"We should find out how many camps there are," said the guard at the tent flap. He had a nice voice.

"The droids said this was camp four," Saché said.

"They appear to be concentrating people based on their jobs," said the guard by the door. "Everyone I've seen in this camp so far has been in some kind of government uniform."

"Where's Bibble?" Mariek asked.

"They took him back to the palace," Yané said. "They probably want him around in case they need someone to send a transmission."

Outside the tent, the construction noises stopped. Mariek went to the entrance and lifted the flap. The whole market was covered with canvas, and she could hear the confused hum of scared citizens. There were droids about, but they didn't seem to care if their prisoners wandered around as long as they stayed away from the charged boundary markers.

"All right," Mariek said. "The camp is set up on a grid system, which makes it easy to divide into quadrants. See if you can get a headcount of each area and a general idea of who's here, and then report back. Oh, and find the water source, too."

"What about the droids? Shouldn't we monitor their patrol patterns and see what we can tell about the defenses?"

"One thing at a time, Sergeant Tonra," Mariek said. "People first, and then we'll worry about the droids."

Saché started toward the tent flap, but Mariek caught her by the collar and pulled her back.

"Not you two," she said. Yané started to protest, and Mariek held up a hand. "I know what you're capable of. I need you to come up with a way to record everything in such a way that the droids won't notice it. You two are going to be the ones to sort through all the information we gather and figure out what we can do with it."

With that, she left them. The two handmaidens stared at each other for a moment.

"Please tell me you put on the under-robe this morning," Yané said. The flame-colored fabric was painstaking to clean, though that seemed less important now. To combat sweat stains, Yané had designed an under-robe of orange Karlini silk. Sometimes the girls went without it, though, because adding an extra layer was too warm.

"I did," Saché said.

"Good," Yané said, pulling her outer robe over her head. "I'm going to need your clothes."

Cleaning carbon scoring off of a droid was nobody's idea of a good time, but Padmé didn't mind. It was worth it to have a reason to hang around the busier parts of the ship, rather than being sequestered with the Queen. That was why Sabé had given her the job, of course, though Padmé didn't for a second doubt that her double was also deeply amused at the situation. They'd all been hired because they could multitask, after all, and if they let despair overwhelm them they would be in real trouble.

Padmé scraped away at the metal for a while before she became aware that she wasn't alone. The Gungan, Jar Jar

Binks, seemed amiable enough. She had never met a Gungan before, and she doubted that Jar Jar could be representative of his whole race any more than she could be of hers, but one ally was a good place to start.

"What do you think, little guy?" she asked the droid that had saved all their lives not that long ago. She spoke too low for Jar Jar to hear her. "Once we're done freeing our planet from the Trade Federation, should the Queen try to make peace with the Gungans? They'll definitely remember her for that."

The blue astromech beeped what sounded like an affirmation, and Padmé smiled at it.

"All right, then," she said. "I'll add it to the list."

⅂⌄⌄⅂

It was nothing personal, but Sabé was really starting to hate Tatooine. The planet was dry, and even with the environmental controls inside the ship, Sabé would swear she could taste the dust. The worst part was that she had to stay in the gigantic black dress, and she could only watch as Rabé and Eirtaé helped Padmé into the plainest outfit they had available: blue trousers and a tunic.

"Do you think the Jedi know?" Sabé asked. "They're supposed to be able to sense things."

"I'm pretty sure Master Qui-Gon is close to figuring it out," Padmé said. "But he hasn't given any indication that he'll stop us."

"He might when you throw yourself into danger," Rabé said.

None of the handmaidens was particularly thrilled with Padmé's plan, and each of them had been sure Panaka would shoot it down. Padmé insisted that he be consulted anyway. Since this involved getting him alone on a very crowded ship, it took some doing, but there wasn't time for any infighting right now.

"Obviously I am not happy about being here," Panaka had said when she asked him. "But you've told me about it instead of just going ahead, and I appreciate that."

"The Jedi might figure it out," Padmé said.

"We can trust their discretion after the fact," Panaka said. "And I understand why you need to see this for yourself. I would feel the same way in your shoes. I do, actually, but there's no way I can get home any sooner without you, so what I'm saying is: please be careful, but I'm in."

"Someone's on the ramp," Eirtaé said, reminding them all of the immediacy of the moment. "We'd better hurry up."

They left Padmé's hair down, lacking the time to finish pinning her braids up. Sabé thought of about a million things to say, and couldn't find the exact words for any of them. She wanted to apologize, wanted to make it right, but they never seemed to have the time. All she could do was accept her place, as she had always done.

"I'll be careful," Padmé promised. "Try to keep busy when I'm gone. It'll make the time go faster."

"I was going to have a chat with that astromech, but they took him along," Eirtaé complained.

"See if you can get the pilot to set up a flight simulator," Padmé suggested. "That won't take too much power."

The girls brightened at the thought of having something to do, but Sabé still reached out for Padmé's hand when she walked by.

"I'll be careful," Padmé promised again, for Sabé's ears alone.

"You better," Sabé said. "This wig itches, and I don't want to wear it forever."

It was almost like normal.

There were about three thousand people crammed into the market square, all of them security or palace personnel. None of the kitchen staff was present, which was alarming, but the droids distributed rations as the sun set, and that was better than nothing. Mariek and Sergeant Tonra put their heads together and came up with something like a duty schedule, since they couldn't all sleep at the same time. Yané and Saché shared a cot.

"I'm sorry," Yané said. There was nothing to unpack, so they just sat awkwardly in the piles of fabric Yané had already salvaged. "I know this makes you uncomfortable."

"I've never . . ." Saché hesitated. Then she bit her lip and kept going. "I've never had to spend this much time with someone I—I mean, I wanted to be professional."

"I understand completely," Yané told her. "But it does feel good to finally talk about this in the open."

"I could have done without the invasion," Saché said. "But yes."

Yané spent the afternoon shredding silk. Even though Saché did what she could to help, Yané made a mess of her hands in the process. The repetitive pressure of tearing silk raised angry red welts in the soft skin between finger and thumb. She washed them as clean as she could and left them open to the air because the only scraps she had to wrap them with were already spoken for. She pushed the thin mattress off their cot, exposing the metal frame, and tied about one-third of the strips longwise, from head to foot.

"It's not much of a loom," she said when she was done. "But it will do."

She put the mattress back on the cot, covering her work,

and shoved the leftover strips of silk underneath the bed. It wasn't much of a hiding place either, but this was a time for doing the best you could.

"We'll weave a code with the rest of the pieces," she explained as she and Saché tried to fall asleep. They were both exhausted from the events of the day, but sleep was hard to come by. "It'll be something simple, like that old comm code we all learned as a memory game when we were kids. Something that the people will understand and the droids will overlook. And because it's under the mattress, it will always be hidden if someone comes into the tent."

It was a good idea, and better than anything Saché had come up with. The stone cobbles were too hard to scratch into, and they didn't even have any chalk, much less a personal device.

"Are you scared?" Yané asked. "You've barely said anything."

"There isn't really anything to say," Saché said. "And yes, I am scared. I don't know what's happened to my family or my friends, and we still don't know if the Queen made if off the planet. I just . . . get quiet sometimes, that's all."

"I know," Yané said. "It's one of the things I like about you."

Saché blushed. In her twelve years, she had never talked so openly about her affections before.

"I know you like to keep your feelings to yourself," Yané

said. "We don't get a lot of privacy, and I respect yours. But I wanted you to know. I do like you."

"I like you, too," Saché said, mostly to the uncaring mattress.

On a dusty world with two bright suns, a little boy looked up from his work and saw an angel.

CHAPTER 19

Saché was sitting near the front of the tent, keeping an eye out while Yané worked, when the Neimoidians came. The situation at the camp had deteriorated rapidly. There was a distinct lack of sanitation and there was never enough fresh water. No one was sick yet, but it was only a matter of time. As expected, food supplies in the city had run low, and the Trade Federation was in no hurry to distribute their own resources. Yané had been weaving nonstop since Mariek started receiving reports, and soon she would have a complete map and guard rotation woven into the silk under their bed.

Saché coughed twice, their prearranged signal, and heard the thump of the mattress landing back on the frame before she breathed again. She didn't look over her shoulder. The tent flap was thrown open, and a droid came in.

"You will come with me," it said. Saché went.

Outside the tent were three Neimoidians. Two she recognized from the initial time Amidala had been captured. Standing behind them, looking dejected, was Governor Bibble. He brightened considerably when he saw that Saché was clearly not injured.

"You Naboo claim to take great pride and care with your children, and yet this one was in the palace when we attacked, and now she is here. It is your fault." Nute Gunray did not become any more impressive the longer he talked. "Will you tell your queen that you cannot protect even a single child in her absence?"

The droid put its metal hand on Saché's neck. She knew exactly how a contest between plasteel and human vertebrae would end, so she didn't struggle. She imagined what it would be like to be truly afraid, and squeezed tears out of her eyes to sell the bit. Mariek appeared out of nowhere behind the visitors, Tonra beside her, but there was nothing either of them could do.

"I will tell my queen anything you like," Bibble said. His eyes cut back and forth between Gunray and Saché, and she knew his words were for her. "I can guarantee that she won't sign the treaty."

"Tell the Queen that the death toll is catastrophic," Saché said. She pitched her voice even higher than normal. There was a good chance the Neimoidians thought she was younger than she was, and fooling them into thinking she was terrified wasn't that hard. She managed another few tears before the droid released her. She fell to her knees and thought that even Rabé would have been impressed with the performance.

"There, Governor, you see?" Gunray said. "Do you think Amidala is so coldhearted that she will ignore that? Your people haven't even *really* started dying yet, and this poor child is already terrified. Come, we will finish our tour of this facility, and then you will send a message to your queen."

They walked off, their droid escort clanking loudly on the stone. As soon as they were around the corner, Saché picked herself up and dusted off her knees. Her robes were starting to smell, and there was no reason to make it any worse. Tonra stared at her with considerable admiration.

"I told you they were good," Mariek said. "Come inside, both of you."

Yané was waiting for them right inside the tent, and she threw her arms around Saché's shoulders.

"Oh, I know there wasn't really anything to be afraid of," she said. "But I was so worried."

"I'm fine," Saché told her. "Bibble is going to send a message to the Queen. That means they survived!"

"What exactly is the Queen going to hear in this message?" Mariek asked, clearly having read between the lines of the conversation even if no one else had. "I don't think we've reached catastrophic levels quite yet."

"*Toll* is one of our alert words," Saché said. "Eirtaé ran some sort of equation and determined that it doesn't come up in conversation very often, so when she hears it, Amidala will know that the message is from me or Yané. She'll know we're alive and that we're doing what we can, and she'll know to stick to her mission."

"I don't think Eirtaé expected us to use it under these circumstances," Yané added. "But Captain Panaka wanted us to be prepared, and so we . . . prepared."

"When they write the official history of this era, I hope they give you some of the credit," Mariek said.

"We're meant to be anonymous," Yané said. "That was the whole point."

They went to the back of the tent and hauled the mattress off of the cot. Yané explained how she had woven the information into her work. Since both Mariek and Tonra had learned the old comm code as children, they saw the pattern immediately. The finished work outlined not only the guard rotation, but also the location of each place where a fountain had been, any entrances to the sewer system, and every power generator that they'd been able to locate.

"We should distribute this to the other tents," Mariek said. "The Queen will come back eventually, and she'll need us. We should be ready to break out if we can, or at the very least, help if we're rescued."

"If I had more material, I could weave a small bit of cloth with the guard rotation on it," Yané said. "That would be enough, don't you think?"

"And I could distribute them while she's working," Saché said. "The Neimoidians already think I'm a terrified child, and the droids never look at me twice."

They spent another half an hour working on the details of

what Yané should put into the fabric. It was decided that any actual escape plan would be need to know. They were mostly soldiers, after all, and soldiers could follow orders. The fabric would contain only the guard rotation, and Saché would give verbal instructions to memorize the information and then destroy the cloth.

"I'm glad you two are with us," Mariek said when they were done planning and Tonra had gone out to see if he could find any spare fabric.

Saché understood the sentiment, but she could still feel cold metal fingers on her neck, and couldn't bring herself to agree.

ꓶꓦꓦꓶ

"It's a trick," said the young Jedi. "Send no reply."

He swept from the room, his brown robe trailing behind him dramatically, and the door hissed shut behind him.

"Well, of *course* it's a trick," Rabé said explosively. "Does he think we're idiots?"

"He thinks we're hiding things from him," Eirtaé said. "And he's correct."

Sabé's face was starting to itch under the makeup. This was the longest she'd ever worn it. At the palace, they used the blend Yané had mixed up, but the stuff that had been stored on the royal ship was a generic brand, and Sabé didn't like it as much. It was a ridiculous thing to be concerned about, she knew, but it was also her *face*, and so she couldn't help it. Being the Queen was starting to get to her.

Also, the starship might have a royal classification, but it had a military-style head, and that made going to the bathroom a logistical nightmare.

She just wanted to go outside and feel fresh air, even if it was sandy and hot. Panaka had forbidden it, and then there had been a sandstorm, anyway; even Sabé wasn't that desperate. She did not enjoy being the person everyone looked to. Even though Rabé and Eirtaé knew who she was, they still had to treat her like the Queen whenever anyone was around, and the distance was off-putting.

This is what it was like for Padmé all the time, Sabé realized. No matter how close to her the other handmaidens got, as soon as the face went on, the walls went up, and Padmé had to trust that when the walls came down again, everyone would still like her. That was why Harli's interest in Sabé had upset Padmé so much. This distance that Sabé couldn't shake any more than she could get her face to stop itching.

"Do you think we should have told him what the message really says?" Sabé asked.

"No," Eirtaé said. "I'm not entirely sure he'd believe you, and in any case, it's none of his business. He's here to negotiate—his master was very clear on that. He can't intercede."

They sat in the silence of their own thoughts for a moment, each conjuring up different fears about what was happening on the planet they had left behind. They knew they had been intended for processing, and that probably meant some sort of relocation camp. The speed at which the camps had been set up meant they weren't likely to be very comfortable, and droids weren't exactly known for their consideration of human frailties. At least the weather was warm.

"I'm glad they're okay," Eirtaé said. "When I heard the word, I almost laughed, I was so relieved."

"I know what you mean," Sabé said.

"And if Saché knew Bibble was sending the message, then that means they know we're all right, too," Rabé said. "Comparatively speaking anyway."

"Panaka said we should have the part by the end of the day tomorrow, or we're never going to get it," Sabé told them. "Master Qui-Gon is going to some sort of cultural event tomorrow morning. He was vague on the details, but he seemed to think he'd be able to take care of everything."

"The Jedi are fine, but I like it better when *we're* manipulating people," Rabé said.

"Agreed," Sabé said. "When Padmé gets back, we'll see what we can do about that."

Even when Sabé wore the Queen's face, it was still in her nature to look to Padmé for guidance. It was something she had missed since their argument after the concert, and something she longed to set right. The galaxy seemed to conspire against them in that regard, but Sabé was determined. If she couldn't find the time, she would simply make it.

ⱶⱵⱵⱵ

Padmé was wide awake, and she felt terrible about it. Qui-Gon and Jar Jar, both self-professed early risers, had volunteered to sleep on the floor in the main room of Shmi Skywalker's house. Shmi had taken her son into his small room and given up her bed for Padmé. It was the most hospitality that Shmi could offer, but the bed was so hard and the desert night so dry that Padmé couldn't sleep.

After an hour of trying not to toss and turn, she got up to get a glass of water. She stepped carefully around the snoring Gungan on the kitchen floor. By the time she had cleaned her cup and put it away, her eyes had adjusted to the dark enough that she could see the outline of Master Qui-Gon, sleeping on his side in the doorway of the house, as though he would protect them from anything that tried to come in.

On the other side of the kitchen, light leaked from under a closed door. Padmé heard soft sounds coming from the other side and wondered if Anakin had gotten up to tinker with something. He really ought to be in bed, so Padmé opened the door to check on him.

"Do you need something?" It was Shmi Skywalker, not

her son, bent over the table with the parts of several different devices spread out in front of her. She was working on some kind of screen.

"I didn't mean to interrupt," Padmé said. "I thought Anakin might have gotten up because he was nervous."

Shmi laughed quietly.

"No, my son sleeps like a rock the night before a race," she admitted. "It's me who stays up all night worrying about him. What's keeping you awake?"

Padmé hesitated. She had already embarrassed herself in front of her host when the topic of slavery had come up, but that was no excuse to stop being honest.

"I am used to a different bed," she said diplomatically. "It is taking me a while to settle."

"You are welcome to sit up with me, if you like," Shmi said. "I'm just trying to fix this screen so I can use it at the race tomorrow."

"I'd like that," Padmé said.

They didn't talk very much after that. Padmé watched as Shmi's clever fingers reassembled the screen, each piece falling into place so easily that Shmi might have been doing magic. It was soothing in the way that watching an artist was, and Padmé realized that this was merely art of a different kind. Eventually, she felt calm enough to try sleeping again, and bid Shmi good night.

As she pulled the blankets over her, Padmé's mind spun.

She'd always known the galaxy was a complicated place, but seeing it, smelling it, *living* it made her understand how foolish and privileged she had been. She had her own problems right now, and they were massive—much bigger than herself. She couldn't afford to be distracted by a planet that wasn't even her own. And yet, her heart ached for this good woman and for her selfless son, and she knew that it always would.

Senator Palpatine's office in the Republic Senate building was fairly standard. He had a high window and a decent view of Coruscant. He could not see the Jedi Temple, for which he was quite grateful. He'd decorated the room with various works of art he'd picked up on his travels as a young man, each piece carefully curated despite the fact that the average museum docent might think them merely a collection of junk. The overall effect was professional and just intimidating enough that he rarely had to host meetings in his own space. He did not want to encourage visitors.

While he waited for the royal entourage to show up, he didn't have a great deal to do. The Senate was stalled on matters he didn't care about, though he was scrupulous at showing up to vote, and he couldn't make any more moves without the presence of the Queen. He was reduced to looking through his catalogue, flicking past entry after entry of artwork he had in storage because he lacked a place to put it.

He froze the screen on a black statue. At first glance, it was barely carved at all and hardly worthy of attention. But if one knew the history of Yonta Prime, and he did, one knew that the deep black surface of the statue absorbed light better than almost any other substance in the galaxy. It was one of his favorite pieces. He had never had the space to keep it anywhere other than his storage facility.

He mentally measured his office. No, it was impossible. The statue would make him look like a careless collector who didn't care for order as long as the piece pleased him. He refused to give in to clutter.

There was an office that would suit nicely, of course. It was a few floors up, and Palpatine had had his eye on it for a while.

He made arrangements for the statue to be packed up and shipped to his residence on Coruscant. He could keep it there for a short while, and then he would have all the space he needed to put it on display.

CHAPTER 20

"I'm going to reach out to the Gungans," Padmé said.

Sabé was still wired from having watched her overthrow the government of the Galactic Republic that afternoon after calling for a vote of no confidence in Chancellor Valorum, so she wasn't entirely sure she'd heard correctly.

"You're going to what?" she said, pulling a comb through Padmé's hair as gently as she could.

The handmaidens were packing the various outfits Padmé had required that day while Sabé put the Queen into her dark purple traveling dress and purple headpiece, and touched up her makeup. It had been a very busy day, and they would have to steal what sleep they could in hyperspace. Sabé was glad to be making this trip in plain robes.

"I'm going to reach out to the Gungans," Padmé repeated. "Jar Jar told me they have an army, right before Senator Palpatine came back. I'm going to ask them to help us."

Sabé considered it. They'd received word that the Jedi would be returning to Naboo with them, but there were only two of them, and Naboo's own security forces were small. The

Gungans did live on the planet, after all. The Trade Federation wouldn't ignore them forever. It was possible they'd already been found. Panaka would be glad of more troops, particularly if they weren't as inherently pacifist as the Naboo.

"Do you think Panaka will be all right with you stepping foot on Naboo as the Queen?" Sabé asked. "It's going to put you in danger, and we'll have to abandon the ship when we land. We wouldn't be able to switch."

"We'll switch before we land," said Padmé. "I was going to tell you what I wanted to say."

Sabé's fingers clenched around the comb. She'd pretended to be the Queen for the first royal tour and the summit's closing remarks, and for the journey here as part of Padmé's safety, but meeting with the Gungans was a huge political step for all of Naboo.

"You were wonderful on the tour and perfect during the summit," Padmé said. "You were so perfect that you covered for *my* mistake when Harli caught me instead of going to her and explaining what happened. You're always going to be in more danger, and it's always going to be your job, but—I trust you. I trust you so much."

"But you're the Queen," Sabé said. "I didn't really understand that until the sandstorm—how isolated that makes you and how you turn that into influence. I was just lonely, but you always find a way to make connections."

"You're as qualified for this job as I am," Padmé said. "If

you wanted to run for the office after me, I think you'd be good at it."

"No," Sabé said. "I wouldn't."

"I don't understand," Padmé said. "There's nothing I can do that you can't."

"There's one key difference between you and me," Sabé told her. "You command, and I carry out."

Padmé didn't reply, so Sabé kept going.

"Do you know why Captain Panaka recruited me?" she asked, somewhat rhetorically. "It wasn't for breathing exercises. We look quite similar, but there must be countless skinny brown-haired girls in the galaxy. He picked me because the thing I am best at, the only thing I have ever been best at, is being *not the best*."

"You're not—" Padmé started.

"No, I am." Sabé cut her off. "I'm good at a lot of things. I work hard and I get results, but I am never the best. And I thought I had accepted that, until Harli looked at me like I was special. And yes, hanging out with her was fun and I did want her to kiss me, but I learned something important that night."

"Not to sneak out of the palace?" Padmé asked.

"Don't be silly," Sabé said. She came around in front of Padmé to check her hair. "That was the best part. What I learned was that I'd rather be second to you than first to anyone else."

Confessing her feelings was like a weight lifting off of Sabé's chest. It had taken her so long to figure it out, to put to words what she knew in her heart. And now she had done it. She wanted to fly.

"I can order you to your death," Padmé said.

Her voice was so quiet that Sabé barely heard her. She reached out and took Padmé's hands.

"And I would go," she said.

"I can't be that dedicated to you," Padmé said.

"I know," Sabé said.

A long silence grew between them, but it wasn't awkward. They both knew where they stood.

"So," said Sabé. "The Gungans."

She separated Padmé's hair and began to braid in preparation for the headpiece.

"Yes," Padmé said. "I wish we knew more about them."

"Well, we know that Jar Jar is an outlier," Sabé said. "That's a start."

"I've been thinking about the summit—how I invited people from all over the sector and not anyone from the species that shares our own planet," Padmé said. Sabé could tell from her tone that she was thinking out loud and didn't interrupt. "In a lot of ways, it's an even thornier problem to try to fix."

"And you're going to start by asking them for help," Sabé said. "That's not going to make it any easier."

She straightened the headpiece on Padmé's head and

turned the chair around for a final check from the front.

"When you talk to them, I think it would be a good idea to be as formal as possible," Padmé said. "We want them to know that they have our respect."

"You mean the Queen's respect?" Sabé asked.

"Yes," Padmé said. "We can work on the rest of it later."

Sabé took Padmé's hands and helped her to step into the purple silk underdress. She sealed all of the seams, and then lifted the dark velvet pieces into place. Once they were fastened, she folded back the heavier fabric to reveal flashes of color.

"What if you spoke with Jar Jar a few more times and let me observe?" Sabé said. "Observe as a handmaiden, I mean. You could ask him questions about Gungan culture. You have a better idea of what we need to know."

"We don't have to switch places until right before we get to Naboo," Padmé said. "So yes, I think that would work."

Sabé did one last inspection of the Queen. Behind her, the others were almost done packing.

"This is a different topic, but I have to ask," Sabé said. "What was it like to overthrow the chancellor?"

"I wouldn't put it like that," Padmé said. "It makes me sound like I fomented open rebellion. I just . . . took advantage of parliamentary procedure while I had the Senate floor."

"You overthrew the chancellor," Sabé said.

"I wish you had seen it." Padmé sounded sad. "So many

people from all over the galaxy, and all they could do was squabble. I told them that our people were suffering, and they would have made us wait until some committee flew out to the Chommell sector and checked. They were more concerned with voting along the lines of their alliance than they were with listening to problems and trying to find solutions. It was a mess, and Chancellor Valorum did nothing. Nothing."

"Do you think a new chancellor will do any better?" Sabé asked.

"I didn't have time to research all of the candidates," Padmé said. "Obviously I would trust Senator Palpatine, and he appears to genuinely like the others. I think any way this turns out, it is in our favor."

"But it won't be in time for Naboo," Sabé said. "No matter what happens in the Senate, we're on our own."

"It will stop the Trade Federation from trying again," Padmé said firmly. "With us or with someone else."

Sabé had a few more doubts about the sanctity of the Republic Senate than Padmé seemed to, but that was why Padmé did things like run for Queen of the planet. She believed in the system, even though she could see its flaws. She would always try to fix them. And Sabé would help her, because that was what she chose to do.

"Are the Jedi joining us on the platform?" Sabé asked. She had trouble keeping track of time on Coruscant. There was always so much ambient light.

"Yes," Padmé said.

"I know we're all worried, but I hope you find time for some sleep on the way home, and I could do with some, too," Sabé said. "If I have to be the Queen again, I am going to need my rest."

Padmé laughed, as Sabé had intended. It was a weak attempt at humor, but it had done the job. The situation was dire, but they could not despair.

"Can I ask a strange question?" Padmé said.

"Of course," Sabé said.

"Did you notice that the face paint was different?"

In spite of everything, Sabé dissolved into giggles, too.

⟓⟒⟒⟒⟒

His master had told him to go straight to Naboo, so straight to Naboo he had gone. The Neimoidians who met him at the palace had fallen all over themselves to make him welcome. They had shown him to a room, and he ignored them.

Instead, he prowled the palace corridors. It was a pretty place, full of bright colors, even when viewed by early morning light. He explored the palace from top to bottom, searching for all the access points. He knew he had a fight coming up; his blood sang with readiness for it. And he was determined to choose the battleground himself.

The hangar near the Royal Palace was the most likely place

for any infiltration force to strike first. He didn't bother to tell the Neimoidians that. They would figure it out or they would not. It didn't really matter to him.

What did matter to him was the series of corridors that led from the hangar down to the power generation facilities. There were two Jedi, which meant they had the advantage of attacking him from multiple directions at the same time. He wanted a way to remove some of those directions, and the maze of catwalks and unguarded pathways in the generator area was perfect for that. He would always know where they were coming from.

At the back of the facility was a series of force fields that opened and shut on a timer. This place would be his ultimate goal. He had a good chance of separating them if he engaged them here, and he was certain he could handle them long enough to lure them all the way down.

He waited until the fields were open and then ran through before they shut again. The room on the other side wasn't perfect for a duel—no room with a hole in the floor that large was ever perfect—but it would do, he decided. Yes, it would do nicely.

He activated both sides of his lightsaber and swung it around, getting used to the feel of the blades this close to the walls. It would be tight quarters. He would be able to bring all his physicality to bear. His master disapproved of so much punching and kicking in his fighting style, but there was nothing better than the feel of bone fracturing under his touch. A lightsaber was nice, but there was something to be said for working with his hands.

He took a flying leap and easily crossed over the chute in the floor. He spared a thought as to where it emerged, and then decided it didn't matter. Soon he would face the Jedi here, and he would bring all his hatred down on them. He was very much looking forward to it.

His comm chimed, and he activated it even though he had no desire to speak to any Trade Federation flunky. His master had told him to play along.

"My lord," said the viceroy. "The royal starship has been detected in the system. It has successfully cleared the blockade and set down in an area of the planet that is heavily forested. We have sent troops out to salvage it, but it is likely the Queen and her party will have fled into the woods. Do you wish to search for them?"

It was tempting. He enjoyed a good hunt. But he had chosen this place to be his battlefield, and was reluctant to give it up.

"No," he said. "Let them come to us."

DETERMINATION
ア ∇Ι ↓ ∇Ι ア ∠ 1 ∩ ⊫ ↓ 1 ∆ ∩

"You keep coming back."

Panaka hadn't seen the girl's legs until she spoke, and then he'd very nearly fallen over them.

"It's a public building," he said. "I can come and go as I please."

"It's a public building that is currently being used to host an acting workshop," she fired back. "For girls."

This was starting to get embarrassing.

"I'm recruiting," he told her.

"It's the middle of the holiday break. The Royal Security Forces have their recruitment at the end of the semester," she said. "No one said anything about rescheduling it."

He didn't bother asking how she knew he was Royal Security. He had a feeling he wouldn't like the answer.

"Do your instructors always tell you when the schedule is going to change?" he asked.

"No," she admitted. "But they say things in front of me a lot. No one really pays attention to me."

Having nearly tripped over her only a few moments ago, Panaka could hardly argue with that.

"The girl you keep turning away from is the best choice," she said.

"I beg your pardon?" Panaka said. He was starting to get used to dealing with child prodigies on a daily basis, but this was asking a lot of his nerves.

"You keep looking at her and making a face like you wish something was different, and then you go back to looking at all the brown-haired sopranos," the girl said. "Picking a blonde would have an advantage."

It was true that the candidate Panaka liked best at the workshop was fair-haired. She didn't seem to care for acting, despite the level of difficulty getting accepted to the program, and was instead dedicating herself to set-building. The other actors assigned to crew positions were all deeply affronted, but she seemed to have chosen it.

"What is the advantage?" he asked.

"If you only pick girls that look like her, she'll never be able to change her appearance without standing out," she replied.

Panaka leaned back against the low stone wall and stared at her appraisingly.

"Who are you?" he asked. "I haven't seen you on stage this week."

"My name is Sashah," she said. "They didn't give me a part and they forgot to assign me a backstage job, and I didn't want to be here in the first place, so I am taking the week to learn more about how people work."

"I think you're doing okay with that," Panaka said. "No one else has figured out what I'm doing, and I've been looking for a week. My name is Panaka."

"Come and see the play tonight," Sashah said. "You'll get to see her in action."

"Oh?" Panaka said. "What sort of action does a set designer see during the performance?"

Sashah smiled. "She's told them several times what they are doing wrong. They haven't listened."

He had to admit that she had piqued his curiosity.

"What about you, then?" he asked. "You must have noticed you look like her."

Sashah considered it briefly and then shook her head.

"I'm too small," she said. "I'm here because my parents thought forcing me to speak in public would do me good, and even that couldn't get me on the stage. You need people who can attract attention and fade into the background. I can only hide."

"You have my attention," Panaka said.

"Only because I spoke to you first," she said. "I always sit here, and this is the first time you've seen me."

"And you gave me excellent advice," Panaka said. "You chose your moment and you took advantage of it."

The girl looked up at him solemnly and pulled her knees up to her chin. She pursed her lips as she considered what he'd said. He appreciated the time she was taking to weigh the options. She knew the stakes, or at least strongly suspected them, and she wasn't going to say yes just because it stroked her ego. She would make sure she was really necessary.

"All right, Captain," she said. He wasn't surprised she had ascertained his rank. "I'll come with you. When do we leave?"

"Tomorrow, probably," he said. "And I imagine there will be three of us."

"I'll get my things," she said. "Do you have a lie prepared for my parents? They're going to wonder where I am if I disappear to Theed."

"Tell them you'll be shadowing a government official," Panaka said. "It's more or less the truth. And tell them that everything else is confidential."

"Very well," she said. "I'll see you tonight, Captain."

She rose to her feet with a dancer's grace and went into the building.

Panaka looked into the alcove where she'd been sitting. It was a good place to be, providing a view of the grounds and yet out of the wind and sun. If she spent a lot of time here, and he imagined she did, she could pick up on a lot of information. She might be small, but her contributions to the Queen's security detail would not be.

The word **small** floated around in his brain for a moment as he stared into the alcove. It was bigger than he'd thought. Definitely large enough that if she sat with her back to the wall, her legs wouldn't reach the stairs.

She'd tripped him on purpose, and then maneuvered him into offering her the job she wanted. Panaka set off for the palace, laughing under his breath. Sashah would fit right in.

CHAPTER 21

Saché was on her tenth trip through the camp when she was caught.

"You there, halt," said a droid, and Saché halted. The tightly folded fabric in the pocket of her ruined orange robes burned against her leg. "Turn around."

The droid was not alone. It was a squad of six, out on patrol. Since their incarceration had begun, the droid patrols had grown more frequent and their methods more violent. Yesterday, three people had been killed for attempting to steal food from the Trade Federation stores, and rations had been cut for everyone as a result.

There had been a fight in Saché's tent when one guard had accused another of hoarding food. Mariek and Tonra had broken it up as quickly as possible. No one wanted the droids to overhear. Mariek assigned the two guards to latrine duty. The original latrines had long since overflowed, and placing new ones was distasteful enough to serve as a deterrent to brawling in the tent. There was only so much Mariek could do, though, so they were waiting for the next blow.

"Your actions are unnecessary," said the droid. "You have no reason to wander through the camp. Explain yourself."

"I don't like being confined to the tent," Saché said. "I was just trying to get some exercise."

"Humans are creatures of habit," said the droid. "If you were exercising, you would take the same path. You do not. Explain yourself."

"I was just looking around." Saché tried to sound as childlike as possible, though the droids had not shown any indication that they cared how old she was.

The droid tilted its head as though it was listening to something or running a calculation.

"Your behavior has been flagged," the droid said. "You will come with us."

There was no point in running. Saché remembered the feel of plasteel against her neck too well to think of resisting either. She tried not to flinch as the droids surrounded her and began a forced march. They were heading for the market office, which the droids had repurposed into a charging station and a small office for the Neimoidian who oversaw operations at the camp.

Sergeant Tonra stood between two tents, an alarmed expression on his face. Saché didn't look at him. He turned and disappeared before the droids could say anything, and Saché knew that word of her capture would get to Yané and Mariek as soon as he could run across the camp with it.

The droids took her into the office and tightened their formation around her so that all she could see was metal torsos.

"Out of the way, you worthless lumps," the Neimoidian overseer said. "How can I interrogate her if I can't see her?"

Saché could think of a couple of ways, but she wasn't exactly going to offer them up. The droids in front of her stepped aside, moving in perfect unison.

"Human children are so small?" the overseer said.

"I'm still growing," Saché told her. "I'm twelve."

"I see." The overseer relaxed back into her chair. "Please, take a seat."

Saché didn't let her guard down, and prepared to press any advantage she gave her. The seat was tall, and her feet hung off the ground, but she made do.

"My name is Usan Ollin," she said. "As you know, I am in charge of this camp. I am alarmed to learn that you are being put in danger."

"I am?" Saché asked. She let her eyes go as wide as she could, and pitched her voice high and a little breathless.

"The adult humans are conspiring against us," Ollin said. "When we have been nothing but considerate since our visit here began. Your queen and her cronies are responsible for this mess. She could end it any time she chose to."

"I know," Saché said. It was always best to mix in as much truth as possible. "But why am I in danger? Is there going to be a food shortage?"

"Well, probably," Ollin admitted. She shook herself. She'd said something she hadn't meant to. "But that's not why you're in danger. The adults are using you, my dear, to carry messages."

"They are?" Saché gasped. "I just wanted to get some exercise."

"I'm afraid so, child," Ollin said. "And you are in very big trouble unless you tell me what the messages say."

"But I don't know." Saché made herself look as innocent and vulnerable as possible and hoped that Neimoidian body language was similar. They cringed a lot, she remembered, and rolled her shoulders forward.

"They thought they were very clever," Ollin said. "They put the information into little scraps of fabric. We found one late last night, and there's another one in your pocket right now. Our droids will crack it eventually. But if you tell me, I'll let you go."

The droids would not crack it. The whole point of the comm code was that it was a memory game for Naboo children that was completely independent of technology. It was like an unsolvable equation or a circular logic puzzle. No computer would be able to crack it without organic help.

"I don't know," she said again. She curled in on herself as much as possible.

"Who gave you the fabric?" Ollin said.

"I—I don't remember," Saché stuttered. "I'm staying with so many strangers and none of them want to talk to me. It's so hard to tell them apart in their uniforms."

"What about the other girl, the one dressed like you?" Ollin said. "My sources say that you were both servants in the palace. Is she a stranger, too?"

"We work together," Saché said. "But I don't see her very much. We have different jobs."

Ollin looked suspicious, but swallowed those two truths and a lie. She leaned forward.

"Child, it is very important that I know what those messages say," she said. "And I think you know more than you are letting on. I'm asking you one more time. For your own sake, tell me who gave them to you."

Saché didn't say anything. The time for bluffing was done.

"Then you leave me no choice," said Ollin. She pressed a button on her desk and the droids clanked back into the office. "Is the interrogation chamber finished, Corporal?"

"Construction is complete," the droid said. "Power has been activated. We have not yet tested the facility."

"I have a test subject for you, then," Ollin said. Two droid hands closed on Saché's shoulders and ripped her from the chair. "I'll upload the questions to your database. Don't stop until she tells you everything."

Saché made them carry her out of the room, though she

doubted her legs would have supported her for more than a few steps anyway. Her brain was trying to stay calm, but her body wasn't listening.

This was probably going to hurt.

Sergeant Tonra burst into the tent without announcing himself or giving the password. Yané threw a bundle of fabric strips into the air and dove for the mattress. Mariek tackled him outright, the two of them crashing to the ground, narrowly missing the edge of the cot that was closest to the door.

"It's me!" he said, and Mariek loosened her grip on him.

"What's happened?" Yané demanded. It had to be bad for the sergeant to ignore all the safety protocols they'd put into place.

"The droids took Saché to the overseer's office," Tonra said. Yané sat down heavily on the cot.

"Do they know?" Mariek asked. For the first time since their incarceration, she looked truly afraid.

"I couldn't tell," Tonra said.

"It doesn't matter if they know," Yané said. "If they suspect enough to take her into custody, they'll want information."

"Saché won't crack," Mariek said. "She's smart enough to go head-to-head with a Neimoidian."

"They built an interrogation room after the executions

yesterday," Tonra said. "They brought in equipment all night. No one could get close enough to see what machinery they have, but several of our people heard the droids talking about it."

Yané made a noise like a wounded nuna. The handmaidens hadn't been trained to withstand physical torture. There hadn't been a reason to. Even Captain Panaka's paranoia didn't extend to blatant cruelty. It wasn't just that, though. Yané didn't want Saché to be hurt by *anything*, ever. Whether she was trained for it or not.

"Let's get as close as we can," Mariek said. "If we stay here, we'll all make ourselves crazy thinking about it."

Whatever rumor mill functioned in the camp was in full force by the time Yané had everything stowed away and they left the tent. Palace guards and staff milled around, knowing that something bad had happened but not having all the details. A few saw Yané by herself and put the pieces together, but one look from Mariek was enough to silence any questions. It was imperative that everyone act as normal as possible.

Droids lined the perimeter of the market office, standing elbow to elbow as though they were expecting to be rushed by attackers at any moment. Their blasters were held at the ready. More droids circulated through the camp, each set of six marching with measured gait as they made sure no one stepped out of line. The tension in the air was palpable. Yané felt it weighing down on her. It was the worst thing she'd ever felt. Saché needed help, and all she could do was wait and hope.

The screaming started after about twenty minutes, and every human in the camp froze. Saché had such a quiet voice. They were used to listening closely to her, to leaning down to catch her full meaning, because so much of what she said was important. The screams were anything but quiet. They were horribly shrill and pierced the air with such ferocity that Yané wasn't sure if Saché was being given the chance to breathe. It went on for several awful minutes, and then it stopped.

The reprieve was short-lived. They must have asked her a question and either she hadn't answered or they hadn't believed what she said. In either case, the result was the same and more screaming filled the air. Yané wanted to vomit. Wanted to plug her ears. Wanted to scream herself to block out the terrible noises. She did none of those things. She could only bear witness to what Saché was doing.

"I'll turn myself in," Tonra said. "I'll tell them—"

"You will not," Mariek told him. "If anyone does anything heroic, it will be me."

Yané had a horrible prescience of telling Panaka that his wife had died, and that snapped her out of her reverie.

"You will not," Yané echoed. She lapsed into the Queen's voice without meaning to, and both guards immediately came to attention. The note of command in her voice was unexpected and absolute. "You will do nothing."

"We have to do something," Mariek protested. "She's screaming."

"If she's still screaming, then she hasn't given them what they want." Yané's eyes ran with tears. She loved Saché and couldn't help her fight the pain. "She is fighting so hard to keep our secrets, and so far she is winning. She knows all she has to do to make it stop is tell them what they want to know, and she is choosing not to do it. We will not unmake that decision for her."

Mariek took both her hands and squeezed.

"You're right," she said. "I hate it, but you're right."

"She just has to hold on a bit longer," Yané said. "Eventually, they'll think she's given them everything she can."

The words were mostly meant as a comfort to herself, but saying them out loud made her feel better. The screaming stopped, cut off like a door slamming shut. Everyone drew a deep breath and let themselves believe that it was over.

But it wasn't.

ᒍᑴᑴᒥ

Her veins and her skin and her bones were on fire and every time the fire went out, the droid asked her to betray her friends. It spoke so calmly and gave such logical arguments. Tell them what they wanted to know, and the fire would stay away. She was tempted. She was so, so tempted. Those few moments when the fire went out became the center of her galaxy.

But there was no choice. Saché picked her friends every time. And the fire burned on.

CHAPTER 22

Mariek watched Yané wrap Saché's hands in the fabric strips she'd been tortured for carrying, and seethed with anger. The droids had released her after three hours of questioning when she hadn't given them anything useful, and Usan Ollin had decided she actually was as ignorant as she claimed. Saché had walked from the interrogation room to the line of droids still guarding the market office under her own power, but it had taken the last bit of will she had. Sergeant Tonra had carried her the rest of the way to their tent.

She was conscious, and it didn't sound like she was in too much lingering pain. Torture devices were often programmed that way so that their victims stayed on the sharp line between pain and relief, and never slid into the buzz of acclimatization. Her body was covered with cauterized lacerations, bright red lines on her hands and face and, one assumed, on her body beneath the nearly ruined orange robe.

"I can sit up," Saché said determinedly, pushing Yané's hands away and pulling herself up to perch on the edge of the cot.

Under the marks, she was pale. Her eyes were bloodshot,

and her voice was hoarse, like the droids had scraped it right out of her throat. But her face was set.

"Who will carry the last few messages?" she asked.

"Tonra will take care of it," Mariek told her. "He's already gone out with the first one. We'll send the rest over the next few hours with different people."

"I have to get back out there," Saché said.

"I am not letting you risk yourself on deliveries again!" Yané said. Her strident insistence surprised everyone.

"I won't have anything on me," Saché said. "I'll just walk randomly through the camp and the droids will watch me."

"What if they take you again?" Yané asked.

"Well, I won't have any incriminating evidence in my pocket this time, so that's a start." The joke fell hollow. "I'll be the distraction. They'll be so busy watching me, wondering what's so important that I am up and moving around already, that they won't look at anyone else. You know I'm right."

"I do," Yané said quietly. She finished wrapping Saché's hand and tucked the loose bit of fabric in so that the bandage would hold. Saché looked down.

"Don't you need these to finish your work?" She held up her hands.

"No," Yané said. "These are spares."

Yané reached under the mattress and pulled out the last four pieces of coded fabric. She handed them to Mariek, who nodded and stepped out to go after Tonra. Yané found a small canteen of water for Saché. They didn't have much, especially with the rations cut, but Saché needed it.

"I'm sorry we don't have anything for your throat," she said.

Saché drank slowly. It made her feel a bit better.

"Oh," she said. "The overseer seemed to think we were headed for a food shortage. She mentioned it and then looked like she wished she hadn't. Our timeline is accurate."

"Hopefully the Queen gets back soon," Yané said. "Or sends a rescue party."

"It would have to be quite a party," Saché said. The attempt at humor caught in her throat and she coughed, wincing. "I have to go. I have to make sure Tonra can get the job done."

Yané knew better than to try to talk her out of it, or even ask if she could come, too. She hadn't left the tent much since they got here, and it was important to continue with behavior the droids would see as normal while the stakes were so high.

"Be careful" was all she said.

Saché gave her a quick hug and then got up from the cot. She was stiff and her muscles protested the move, but she wasn't going to be deterred. One foot after another, she walked to the tent flap and ducked through.

It was the same as every other walk she'd taken across the camp, to tell the truth. She didn't make eye contact with anyone and stayed out of the way of the droid patrols, ducking to the side every time she met one. She went into tents at random, holding up a hand for silence when she encountered other prisoners. She circled back to Yané, stayed with her for half an hour, and then went back out.

It was three hours before the droids stopped her the first time.

"Human," the droid said. Saché flinched, and it was real. The droid motioned to one of its counterparts. "Search her."

Saché endured it. The metal hands pawed at her, turning out her pockets and feeling for protrusions under her robes. They found nothing, and let her go. Saché's steps were shaky, but she made it all the way around the corner before her legs gave out. Even then, sitting on the cobblestones, she didn't give voice to the scream she'd felt starting to boil in her stomach when the droid had touched her. She took a deep breath, pushed herself to her knees, and then her feet, and kept walking.

The droids stopped her three more times before the sun set and curfew began. Each time was a test of wills fought inside Saché's chest: the will to scream and the will to not. Not won, and every time the droids were forced to let her go on her way, it became easier. The last droid, the same corporal who had arrested her that morning, sent her back to her tent as the light fled.

Yané was waiting for her by the door and pulled her into a hug as soon as she entered. Mariek hugged her, too, and Tonra squeezed her shoulder lightly enough that he didn't aggravate her burns. Yané pulled her to the back of the tent and laid her out on the mattress. For the first time that day, Saché gave in to oblivion.

This was the simplest royal outfit in the Queen's wardrobe. Sabé was able to get into it herself, except for the broad waistband, which fastened at the back. Padmé had sealed the seam herself, determined to do everything she could to protect her friend even as she thrust her into danger.

"There will be more than enough danger to go around," Sabé said, guessing what Padmé was thinking.

"I didn't want a war, and yet I took the first chance I had to fight," Padmé said. "I'm even going to try recruiting an army. I didn't like the hypocrisy in the Senate, but it turns out that I am just as bad."

"You're really not," Sabé said. "You are defending your planet in a desperate moment, and you are being very, very deliberate about the steps you take. There is nothing shameful or hypocritical in that."

Padmé helped her into the surcoat and straightened the lines on her sleeves.

"Is there anything you want to review?" Padmé asked. "We can go over your speech again, if you like."

Sabé took a deep breath and looked at herself in the

mirror. The headdress was already in place. All she had left to put on were her sturdy boots.

"I think I'm as ready as I can be," Sabé said. "I'm nervous, but I'll do you proud."

Padmé took her hand and squeezed it.

"I know you will," Padmé said. "Whatever happens, I know you will."

"I'm ready for you, Padmé," Rabé said from across the room. She and Eirtaé were dressed in gold and maroon, like Padmé was, and both of them had their hair up already.

Padmé sat down and let Rabé arrange her hair. There wasn't a lot Eirtaé could manage for defense on short notice, but Rabé had borrowed some concussive-absorbing material from the lining of one of the Queen's dresses, and she used that to tie up everyone's hair. It wouldn't do anything to stop a blaster bolt, but it would provide some protection against a heavy blow or a falling piece of debris, and that was better than nothing.

"We're about to come out of hyperspace." Pilot Ric Olie's voice came through the ship's communication system. "Everyone be prepared to evacuate as soon as we land."

There were two other maroon dresses laid out, with hair ties ready to go. None of them said anything about it, but every one of them hoped.

Panaka made his way through the Theed sewer system until he reached the pipe that led to one of the fountains in the market square. He had not been able to do as much reconnaissance as he wanted. Since they landed and evacuated the royal ship so quickly, he had a limited number of resources to work with. They had only been able to take very fast scans of the planet when they were coming in to land, and that was how he'd known there was a prison camp just inside the city wall. He hoped it would contain the people he was looking for.

There were a few obstacles he had to remove, all of them designed to keep people *in*, not out. The Theed sewer system was the only part of the planet's infrastructure that was completely run by droids—for health purposes—and therefore it was flooded all the time. There were emergency releases to drain each cloaca, but they could only be used sequentially, starting from the sewage treatment plant outside of the city. This explained why no one in the camp had tried to use the tunnels to escape. The situation couldn't be comfortable, but if they weren't taking major risks, then that meant it hadn't deteriorated too badly yet.

He climbed the ladder and then extended a sensor through the sewer cover. It was dark, but he had no idea what he was climbing into. At least this way, he would be able to avoid any droids.

The coast was clear. He tested the strength of the sewer cover. It was stone, held in place by a carved ledge. All he had to do was push it straight up and it would start moving. Getting it far enough to the side that he could crawl out without making too much noise would be the challenge.

He braced himself on the rungs, hunched over under the cover, and then pushed up. The cover shifted upward, and he painstakingly pulled himself up another rung so that he would have more leverage. Once he cleared the ledge, he leaned backward to move the cover onto the ground. It hurt tremendously, and he was very glad that he was wearing his leather coat. After an agonizing moment where he was balanced on his toes and leaning backward with a huge weight on his neck, the center of gravity shifted to be over the ground instead of over the hole, and he breathed out a sigh of relief.

He climbed up and then hauled the cover back on. He didn't know how long he would be here, and it wouldn't do anyone any good if the droids found his egress. He made his way through the camp, his hat pulled down over his face, until he saw a guard he recognized posted outside a tent. She was sitting down, working on fixing a boot, but he could tell she was keeping watch for something. He smiled.

The palace guard on watch in front of Mariek's tent was quite surprised to see her commanding officer.

"Captain!" she said, remembering at the last moment to keep her voice down. She stood up quickly. "How did you—"

The expression on his face silenced her. The practicalities were neither here nor there. With a crisp salute, the guard lifted the tent flap, and he strode through.

Panaka had eyes for only one person.

"I'm so glad you're all right," he said as Mariek froze in surprise and then threw herself into his arms. "I was told the girls are here, too?"

"Yes," Mariek said. She squeezed him one more time and then let him go. "They're okay."

Saché had woken up in all the fuss and came over to say hello. She certainly didn't look okay, and Yané looked worried about her, but Panaka trusted his wife's judgment for the moment.

"We can't all go," Mariek said once Panaka explained that he had cleared the sewer tunnels enough for an escape. "It's impractical, and it would ruin the element of surprise."

"How many people do you think we can sneak out to be beneath the droids' notice?" Panaka asked. "We'll have to prioritize pilots if we're going to be leaving people behind."

"A few dozen, maybe," Tonra said. "If we spread it out between the tents, that might give us a bit more to work with."

"How would we even start to coordinate that?" Panaka said.

"We already have, Captain," Yané said. "Every tent has a

map of the camp and a log of the guard rotation. They just need a direction to go and orders to get there."

He looked between her and Saché, and then to Mariek.

"I'll explain it later," his wife said. "We have to move."

Since their tent would be losing runners on a one-way trip to activate the other groups, it was decided that only Mariek, Tonra, Yané, and Saché would go with Panaka. The runners were dispatched, and Panaka led the way back to the sewer cover he had used earlier. They waited for the first set of escapees to arrive, and then four of them lifted the cover together. It was much easier that way. He sent Mariek ahead with Yané and Saché, and then stayed with Tonra until everyone who was leaving in the first wave had made their descent. Four palace guards stayed behind to put the cover back into place, a last-minute decision that Panaka didn't like, but his subordinates had insisted. Then, with their tracks covered up as well as they could manage, the escape was underway.

Saché walked even though she was exhausted and wanted nothing more than to sleep. There was no promise of rest at their destination, but there was no way she was staying in the camp any longer than she absolutely had to. She didn't want to get hemmed in by droids ever again.

They exited the sewer through a grate that went into one

of Naboo's many lakes. Several landspeeders waited there, and Panaka ferried them back to the place where the Queen's party had established themselves. Panaka told them about the plan to talk to the Gungans, and how they had to wait for their emissary to return. And then Saché saw bright gold stripes that lined the handmaiden's outfits in the dark and knew that she was truly safe. The Queen maintained some distance, of course, but Padmé was close enough to get a good look at them.

Saché could tell she had a hundred questions and probably even more apologies, but now was not the time for any of that. Instead, when Padmé held out her arms, Saché hesitated for a moment—too aware of her own smell—and then wrapped her arms around her.

"I'm so glad," Padmé said. "I'm so glad."

Eirtaé and Rabé hugged them as well. Saché wanted to laugh and cry at the same time. It was possible that she was finally going into shock. She and Yané splashed their faces in the creek and tucked away their hair. When they were as clean as they could manage, they changed into the maroon and gold battle uniform the others wore. Sabé took their hands, which was as much as she could do while she wore the Queen's face. They were together again, and Padmé Amidala had a plan.

The Trade Federation didn't stand a chance.

CHAPTER 23

The moment Padmé stepped in front of her, Sabé knew that she had failed. Sabé was always supposed to stand between the Queen and danger, and not only had she faltered in her task, she had stood there and gaped as Padmé walked forward. It was her moment, and she had let it slip right through her fingers.

They had practiced as much as they could. She'd observed Jar Jar, and she and Padmé had hammered out exactly what to say. She'd never been more nervous in her life than when she stepped forward to address Boss Nass, and she had delivered what she knew was a perfect performance of everything she had prepared.

And it hadn't been enough. Padmé had stepped in and changed the script. It was brilliant of her, of course, to change so quickly once she realized what Boss Nass wanted to hear, but it had also exposed her in front of everyone, and that was something Sabé was supposed to avoid at all costs.

She never wanted to get up from her knees, but of course she had to. When Padmé rose, smiling with Boss Nass's approval, Sabé followed suit. At least now she might be able to get out of the Queen's makeup and dress.

"It wasn't your fault," Padmé said. She came over to where Sabé was sitting on a log, which wasn't queenly at all. At least as herself, she could slouch. "You did exactly what we planned."

"And it wasn't enough," Sabé said. "I could have been better. If I were more like you, I would have seen that it wasn't working and reached the same conclusion you did. I could have talked to him the same way."

"But it wouldn't have been the truth," Padmé said. "And in that moment, we needed the truth."

"You know, most of the time I'm okay with being second best," Sabé said. She looked at Padmé and saw her friend's face, not the Queen's disappointed understanding. "You get invited to all the fancy parties and you rarely have to speak in public. There's never any pressure on you. That's what it's like being Amidala. I just try to be you, and that's all anyone will remember. But sometimes I know I could have done better, and by the time I've figured out how, it's too late. I hate that. I feel like I failed you."

"And I feel like I failed you," Padmé said. "We only prepped one speech. I should have been more flexible when we were getting ready."

Sabé straightened.

"I hadn't thought of it that way," she admitted.

"It's in our natures to blame ourselves, I think," Padmé said. "That's definitely one way we are the same."

"Do you want to change?" Sabé asked. "We'll have to do it fast."

"There isn't time," Padmé said. "Captain Panaka wants to get moving right away. And even if we had time, I need you to be the Queen for a bit longer. We have to take the throne room, and if there's any way you can be a distraction again, we should use it."

Sabé nodded, a bit disappointed. The decoy maneuver was exciting, but after holding the character for so long, she longed to be herself again. It was ridiculous to put her personal wishes first in such serious circumstances, but she couldn't entirely help it.

"Sabé," Padmé said seriously. "You might die."

"I know," Sabé said. "That's always been part of the job."

"But it's for real this time," Padmé said. "Before, if we died we were all going together, blown up on the royal starship or something. But you'll be alone. You'll be exposed. And you'll be Amidala."

"I know," Sabé said.

"I want to be noble and tell you I won't order you to do it," Padmé said. "But that would be cowardly, too, and you deserve better than letting me make a martyr of you."

"I appreciate that," Sabé said. It was strange to talk about this out loud after turning it over in her head so many times, but it was remarkably freeing to hear Padmé say it out loud. "My hands are yours."

And they always had been.

Gregar Typho had not been in Theed when the invasion came. His leave had begun as soon as the summit was concluded, so he'd gone home. His uncle and aunt Panaka were supposed to follow him a few days later, assuming his uncle could be talked into leaving the Queen, but of course that hadn't happened.

Instead, Typho had spent the Occupation in camp three, which was mostly populated by civilians who had been incarcerated in the campus dormitories of Gallo Mountain University. Sanitation and fresh water hadn't been an issue, but food ran short almost immediately, and Typho divided his time between protecting his family and making sure that the children in the camp had as much food as he could manage to scrounge for them.

The Trade Federation hadn't bothered to scan the dorms before installing their prisoners, assuming that everyone who attended higher education on Naboo was an artist or a philosopher. Typho was able to find a working transmitter almost immediately, and assigned shifts to people he could trust to monitor communication channels in case someone broke through. As his fellow prisoners weakened under the food shortage, he took on a few shifts himself, and it was he who was on duty in the early hours when the call finally came through. The Queen was back, and resistance was finally possible.

Gregar Typho rubbed the grit from his eyes and got ready to fight.

꒤꒨꒨꒤

Sabé hovered in the back of the briefing while Panaka outlined their plan for what she'd already started to think of as the Battle of Naboo. There would be three fronts. The Gungan army would meet the bulk of the droids on open ground outside the city. It was the force that had been trying to exterminate them, so the Gungans were itching for a fight. The second front would be in space. Panaka and the Jedi would get the pilots to the hangar, and get as many of them as possible into the air, before moving on to take the throne room. The third front would be in the city itself. Once the fighting began, a splinter force led by Mariek Panaka would rally whatever Naboo citizens they could find and try to spread word of what was happening in the city via the short-range comms.

It was almost a relief that everyone present knew she was a fraud. If she'd still been playing Amidala, she would have been at the front, trying to coordinate Padmé's facial expressions into a proper response. It was much easier this way, to observe and worry about protecting the Queen later. Panaka dismissed them to make last-minute preparations, and Sabé wandered a few steps away from the main group to gather her thoughts.

"What's your name?" someone asked. She turned. It was Anakin Skywalker, looking at her quite directly. Neither of the Jedi had asked.

"Sabé," she told him. There was no reason to keep it a secret. He would leave and she would probably never hear of him again.

"It's good to meet you, Sabé," he said. "Thank you for keeping her safe."

Qui-Gon called out for him, and he wandered off. Sabé was oddly touched.

The handmaidens gathered together while Padmé discussed the final few details with Panaka and the Jedi. They'd all been given blasters for the coming battle. They had been trained in both close and ranged combat, but none of them felt particularly prepared.

They'd all seen the marks on Saché's skin, but she hadn't volunteered anything about them, and they were reluctant to ask. Instead, Rabé had told them about everything that had transpired on Coruscant. They tried to fill the time, but there was nothing any of them wanted to say. All they could do was wait for their marching orders.

At last, the final battalion of Gungans departed for the grassy plain where they would make their stand. The rest of them got into speeders and headed for the capital.

Whatever happened, they were going to reach the throne room.

CHAPTER 24

The battle plan fell apart almost immediately. No sooner had the pilots made their escape than a dark figure with a red blade had appeared in the hangar, blocking the main access to the palace. Padmé declared they would take the long way and left the Jedi to their fight. Sabé didn't want to be anywhere near the person who was attacking them, but she was also worried about leaving them behind. Without the Jedi, the plan to take the throne room became more complicated.

The two teams split up, with Sabé heading through the palace gardens and Padmé taking the corridors. Sabé tried not to think about how the others were doing. She knew the Jedi could probably handle themselves, but the Gungans faced truly overwhelming odds and were entirely reliant on the Naboo pilots knocking out the control ship as soon as possible. She focused on the droids in front of her, the feel of her blaster in her hands, and moved up through the palace as quickly as possible.

"Sabé!"

Someone called her name, and Sabé turned to see Rabé's group down a corridor that should have been off their route. The group was too small: Padmé wasn't with them. Sabé got the attention of her party and brought the two groups together.

"Report!" she said, deciding that was what the absent Panaka would do.

"They're okay," Rabé said. "We got pinned in a hallway, and they took ascension cables as a shortcut."

A weight lifted off Sabé's chest.

"There are a lot of droids in the palace, even with the Gungan maneuver," a guard informed them. "We are still trying to get to the throne room in case they need us."

"In case she needs me," Sabé said. "Our route has been busy, but not too bad. Come with us."

Sabé would do whatever it took. This time, there would be no room for mistakes. If she was called to be the Queen, she would have to act immediately. She had never been more scared of anything in her entire life.

Anakin Skywalker liked flying.

Mariek and Tonra pelted up the stairs to the towers that surrounded the market square. They knew from Yané's weaving which tower had droids on the lowest charge at this time of day, and that was their target. It was an ugly fight, as blaster bolt exchanges at close quarters always were, but the two of them managed to get the drop on the droids. From there, they took control of the tower's gun and blasted the other lookout points to smithereens.

It wasn't a prearranged signal, but the guards still in the camp knew to expect something eventually, and the destruction of Trade Federation property was a pretty obvious call to action. At considerable risk, they charged the battle droids, hoping to strike them from an angle where their bodies were the weakest and immediately salvage the blasters. Most of them were successful, though none of them escaped without at least minor injury.

Usan Ollin stood in the doorway of her office, shrieking orders at droids who were too busy to pay attention to her. Mariek saw the opening, and it was too tempting to pass up. Leaving Tonra in charge of the gun, she ran down the stairs to the main camp and crossed the ruined market square one last time. She could have stopped for a blaster, but she didn't. Instead, she tackled the droid closest to Ollin and, when the clanker went down, punched the overseer right in the face.

Anakin Skywalker *really* liked flying.

When Captain Panaka implemented the handmaidens as Queen Amidala's personal guard, he introduced a high number of moving pieces to a very high-stakes field of play. He had his methodologies, the Queen had hers, and the handmaidens each brought something different to the table. It could have gone very badly, but the girls worked hard and adapted to each scenario they encountered. It wasn't a perfect system, not yet, but they had all quickly settled into their roles.

He'd selected Tsabin because she was used to being second best. She was used to people looking right through her while she played her part. She was used to being out of the spotlight and out of everyone's mind. Tsabin had tried to convince the Gungans to join their fight, and Tsabin had failed. Sabé was determined that it would be the last time.

When she got to the throne room, she surveyed the scene quickly. Her heart sank. There were too many droids. Nute Gunray had Padmé, and he thought she was Amidala. They were outgunned and overwhelmed, but had reached their primary objective. They were in the throne room. All Padmé needed was a moment. A distraction.

A decoy.

Sabé moved before she was finished thinking it through. She left the relative safety of the guards who surrounded her and ran toward the throne room. They followed her, as she knew they would. She stood in full view of the Neimoidians and their droids.

"Viceroy!" she called out in the Queen's voice. "Your occupation here has ended."

And then she ran.

She went back through the line of guards, steps pounding on the marble floor of the hallway as the droids came after her. She was moving so fast the headpiece she wore slid loose of its pins and canted backward on her head. She heard the hiss-slam of the blast doors sealing the throne room shut and knew that her desperate ploy had worked. The droids were on her side of the blast doors, and Padmé was on the other, the royal pistol in her hands. All Sabé had to do now was stay alive.

The droids had followed her without doing a tactical analysis of what she was running toward, and slammed straight into the wall of guards. By the time Sabé was able to turn around, most of the droids were down. She took out one of them, and then the blaster fire was silenced. In the quiet, she could hear her heart pounding. She had no idea what was really happening in the throne room. She just had to trust that everything had gone as she hoped.

Padmé Amidala stood victorious in her throne room with the viceroy at her mercy and the planet back under her control. She lowered her blaster and looked around the room. There was carbon scoring on the floors and scrape marks from where metal had been dragged over marble. A few of the art installations had been destroyed, and more than one window was broken. The rest of Theed was probably the same way, but there would be time for that after she discussed the new treaty.

The buildings were damaged, but they were fixable. The people were hungry, but they could be fed. And once again, Naboo was theirs.

CHAPTER 25

The first thing they had to do was bury the dead.

The Gungans took their fallen warriors to their sacred place. Amidala was invited to go and witness the funeral, but there was no time. She sent Eirtaé and Yané, who both gave a full report of the moving ceremony when they returned.

The Naboo dead were sent to their family burial plots or interred in the city cemetery. Everyone who perished in the battle would have the Queen's crest carved into their headstone, and Padmé decided that one year later, she would do a tour of the planet to see the finished stones and hold memorials.

The droids were salvaged and melted down. They were made of high-quality materials. They would be remade into fence posts and garden trellises and art.

Qui-Gon Jinn was laid out on a pyre by the waterfall on the cliff at the end of the river. They waited to burn him until the Jedi Council arrived to witness his funeral. The newly elected Chancellor Palpatine would be arriving with the Jedi, and Padmé looked forward to offering her congratulations almost as much as she was looking forward to turning Nute Gunray over to Republic justice.

A Jedi funeral was a solemn affair, and Padmé knew that it was a great honor for the Naboo to be trusted to see to his remains. She wore the dark purple dress again, but this time instead of Sabé's hands alone, those of all of the handmaidens dressed her. Yané arranged the headpiece and Rabé did her makeup. Saché polished her shoes and Eirtaé sealed the seams up her back. Sabé turned the heavy velvet down to let the lighter silk show through, and Queen Amidala was ready to mourn.

The ceremony itself was simple. No one spoke, except quietly amongst themselves. Instead they watched as Qui-Gon's body was lit up in bright fire, and they kept watching until he had been reduced to ash. Padmé's grief felt more personal than she had expected. The Jedi Master had trusted her when he knew she was keeping secrets, had let her try to keep control of a wildly unpredictable situation, and had respected her judgment enough to at least listen to her arguments. She would never get to thank him for any of that. They would never look back at what they had experienced together and find the lighter side of it. It would always be an open wound.

The Jedi drifted away from the pyre alone or in pairs, mysterious and sad in a way that defied description. Obi-Wan and Anakin stayed until the last ember burned out, and so did the Queen and her court. The night air was chill and they were all exhausted, but it was the best way to show their thanks to the soft-spoken Jedi Master who had risked much and given all to save their home.

When the music had finished and the flower petals were swept from the square, Queen Amidala and her handmaidens gathered on the balcony where the Trade Federation had first captured them. The Jedi were gone, and Anakin Skywalker had gone with them. Most of Naboo would never know what he had done for them, but those who did know would never forget.

Sabé had brought her hallikset outside with them. She hadn't played it in months, but opening the case was like going home. She fitted the pieces together and checked her tuning. Once, the instrument had been her obligation. Her task. Her duty. Once, the music she played had filled her heart while the knowledge of her shortcomings had drained it. But she knew better now.

With her friends around her and the clear Naboo sky above, she started to play.

The girl in the white dress had her mother's brain and her father's heart, and a spark that was entirely her own. Brilliance and direction and compassion as bright as the stars. But now she was alone, and no one could help her. Whatever happened next, however it was recorded and remembered, she was entirely on her own.

From the time she was small, she had wanted to help. Her father was often gone offworld, and it wasn't until she was sixteen that she tried to take action on her own. It hadn't ended particularly well, but she had learned a valuable lesson and gained the trust of her parents in the process. When she'd stood at the top of Appenza Peak, her planet stretching out from her in beautiful blues and greens as far as she could see, she had known she would never see anything quite so beautiful as home.

She'd always known that it had been her great privilege to be adopted into her family, and what it would mean for her when it was time to take her mother's place on the throne. She'd worked hard to be worthy of it, even the parts she didn't like. She'd given up her dignity and her freedom and, once, a boy she'd loved, and she'd known every time that she would do it again for the people she would someday rule.

But now—now she would never live her parents' dreams for her. She would never rise as high as they had hoped she would. The throne was gone and the mountain was gone and they were gone, and it felt like she was the only one left. But she wasn't about to let that stop her.

The more she thought about it, the more she realized that running a rebellion and running a planet were not as different as she'd thought. Both required a sacrifice of self, and both required an understanding of being a small part in a larger whole. The Rebellion's hope was strong, but their list of allies was thin. She knew she was up to the challenge.

And now she stood alone, even though she was surrounded by people in the hall. She could even see other Alderaanians in the front row, standing proudly at attention as though their souls weren't crushed by the weight of a loss that was next to impossible to quantify. The battle was done and they would celebrate it. But in her heart, she knew that the war would be long. She always had. She had made herself to fight, and she would do so for as long as she drew breath.

The music began, and the huge doors at the back of the hall slid open to reveal the Heroes of the Rebellion. Suddenly, she didn't feel quite so alone anymore.

The girl in the white dress was never going to be Queen, but she was ready.

ACKNOWLEDGMENTS

Thanks, as always, to Josh, who called within ten minutes after I emailed him all, "Hey, do you think we could get a *Star Wars* book?" one cold December morning in 2014. It had a different title and, um, plot back then, but the heart was the same, and Josh helped me see it through.

Jen Heddle remains extraordinary, in case anyone is keeping score. Thank you for always letting me take risks and then making sure I stick the landing. And for that scene where we made sure someone's going to have to add a menstruation page to Wookieepedia. What's next?

Lucasfilm Story Group remain some of my favorite people, even if I don't ask specific enough questions, resulting in Leland giving me eight named planets (what I'd asked for) and then Pablo telling me there are in fact SEVERAL DOZEN PLANETS. Matt's notes always make me laugh. Emily, I am probably going to tell too many people that I was right about the pilots, so feel free to remind everyone that I literally cannot ever remember what any of the ships are called.

Leigh and Tara, you've made my words look beautiful (again!) and I am so, so pleased with the whole package. Here's to many, many dresses.

Michael Siglain, Lyssa Hurvitz, Dina Sherman, and the rest of Team Space Mouse, thank you for getting the word out. To my fellow *Star Wars* writers: it's a pleasure as always to share this galaxy with you and borrow cool things. I didn't break Panaka. That's on Claudia.

Emma, as always, I think I'm Force-sensitive.

Davis, you liked *The Phantom Menace* and I breathed a sigh of relief. I love you so much. Your enthusiasm for *Star Wars* bolsters my joy whenever I think about it.

And, finally, thanks to Dot, who jokingly renamed My Chemical Romance at exactly the right moment in my life. It was destiny, I guess.

Queen's Peril was begun in the author's head in 1999, written in September of 2019 in a fog of *Mindhunter* and *My Little Pony*, and edited quite ruthlessly all across North America.